ONCE UPON AN ISLAND

Another You Say Which Way Adventure
by:

By DM Potter

ISBN-13:978-1519257697
ISBN-10:1519257694

How This Book Works

- This story depends on YOU.

- YOU say which way the story goes.

- What will YOU do?

At the end of each chapter, you get to make a decision. Turn to the page that matches your choice. **P62** means turn to page 62.

There are many paths to try. You can read them all over time. Right now, it's time to start the story. Good luck.

Oh … and watch out for the giant squid!

Once Upon an Island

A little into the future.

The arms of the giant squid slither and tighten around you. You struggle to pull yourself free, but the squid is strong. You gasp for air before it tugs you down into the depths of the sea. You hold your breath, but how long will you last?

How did you end up like this? If only you'd made different choices. If only you could start again.

Wait a minute – you can!

You are about to enter a story that depends on YOU. You make the decisions. You shape the story. It's up to you, so what will you do?

Here is how it starts – but you will decide how it's going to finish.

You have been invited to New Zealand to spend the school holidays with your cousins, Stella and Max. They are going to stay on an island called Arapawa. If you don't want to go, you can stay with your mother's friend.

It is time to make your first decision. Do you:

Go to Arapawa Island? **P2**

Or

Stay with you mother's friend. **P8**

2

You have decided to go to Arapawa Island.

Out of the airplane window the sun is rising over a large green land surrounded by an aquamarine ocean. There are rolling hills, forests, and lakes. The plane touches down and in no time you are meeting your cousins, Max and Stella.

Both have thick dark hair and large green eyes. Dressed in t-shirts and shorts they definitely look like brother and sister.

Together you head to a ferry to sail to the top of the South Island. From there you will take a smaller boat to Arapawa Island.

The ferry is huge with cars on the bottom level, a playground and shops in the middle, and a movie theatre and restaurants on the top. There is a jerk as the ferry leaves the port but no real feeling of movement yet as it glides further into the harbor. The harbor is large and filled with other boats ranging from massive container ships to small sail boats. Tall city buildings cluster on the flat ground between sea and hills. Around them are green hills, and here and there you see colorful houses stacked along steep, curving streets. The ferry leaves the shelter of the harbor and enters 'Cook Strait', and you feel the strong engines beneath your feet crank up the pace as the vessel starts to move up and down in the ocean waves.

You get lockers for your luggage and then take a stroll around the boat, getting to know each other again – it has been a while since you were together.

Max and Stella are twins. They are the same age as you. They ask you about your home and school and family. Then it's your turn: "What are you guys into now?" you ask. The two of them look at each other wondering perhaps what to say, Stella begins:

"I've been working after school at a bird sanctuary for two years. I show people around and take care of some of the animals and birds. I'll be keen to see what's roosting on Arapawa."

"And you think you might do some diving too," cuts in Max. "She's a fantastic swimmer and won the regionals this year. We think there might be places around the island to do some snorkeling and maybe free dive to find shipwrecks."

Max explains that he likes drawing and riding his dirt bike, and he plays guitar and trumpet. He wishes he could have brought the bike to the island.

They tell you what they know about the island you are travelling to. The water is very deep on one side of Arapawa Island – great for fishing off the rocks, but probably quite dangerous for swimming.

"I'm not afraid of deep water!" you say.

"It's not so much the deep," Stella says ominously. "It's what is *in* the deep."

The ferry is well out to sea now and the rise and fall from the waves makes walking around strange. Sometimes the floor meets your feet too soon and sometimes it falls further than you expected. The cafeteria is full of people doing the

4

same unbalanced walk as you. You slide trays along a bench, picking your food from cabinets above – there are sandwiches, hot savory pies, sausage rolls, and fries. Stella has the money for food and she chats with the man who serves you as she pays.

"Is it going to be a rough crossing?" she asks.

"No, love, it's only rough going out the heads." As the crewman says this you notice with envy the easy way he holds himself as the ship moves.

You lurch between tables, looking for somewhere to sit – it's hard to balance a tray of food on a boat, and you all stagger about trying not to spill your lunches.

At the back is a big table with just one person sitting at it. He is reading a newspaper. Max asks the man if it would be okay to share the table, and he grunts and shuffles his chair across to make room. He lifts up the paper and hides behind it. The headline reads "Tuatara missing from sanctuary". What, you wonder, is a tuatara?

Then you remember something else you were wondering about.

"Who is the woman we are staying with, Max?" Things have happened so fast that you haven't had a chance to find out much about your host.

"Madeline – we call her Aunt Maddy," Max says. "She's an old friend of our parents, not really our aunt. She lives on the island when she isn't teaching science at a university. We went to the island with our parents when we were young – I don't remember too much, though. Aunt Maddy is very nice but a bit eccentric. I think she'll be happy to let us do our own thing."

You are about to ask about the missing tuatara, but then you see that a woman at the next table is sneaking food into a large handbag that's sitting on the chair beside her. A snout and a pink tongue emerge to take the food. The woman tries to close her bag but she is too late – the head of a fox terrier rises up to inspect the table. It wears a red leather collar with an odd pendant dangling from it.

You aren't the only person who noticed the dog – a steward comes over and glares at the woman.

"You can't have a dog loose on board," he says. "It will have to be caged or stowed in a car below deck."

The little dog yaps at the steward.

"Shhh, Trixie!" its owner says. "I'm sorry. I'll go and put her in my car right away."

Later, you are all on deck when the boat slows as it enters a wide channel with land on both sides. The water is much calmer. The ferry begins to pass Arapawa Island and the three of you hang over the rail to look at the place you'll be going. You pass some little harbors and inlets with boats in the water. There are a few houses near the coastline. The hills seem to be mostly pasture near the sea, but further up there are places covered in trees.

"Some people farm there," says a nearby passenger to his friend. "Or there are people who have weekend houses that they get to by boat."

"The fishing must be out of this world from that island," his friend muses.

You look at the island and don't see any roads, just a few tracks.

"Those tracks would be fun to explore on a dirt bike," Max says wistfully.

"It's a pity you don't have your bike then," Stella says. "I guess your legs might be an alternative way to do it."

The two of them start arguing good-naturedly. Then Stella gives a shout and points out a small harbor.

"Maddy's house is there," she says.

"Do you remember it from when you were young?" you ask.

She laughs. "No – I looked it up on Google Earth."

You see an old fashioned yellow house a short way up the hill, and some farm buildings above that. There is a sailboat tied up to the jetty.

"Looks like Maddy hasn't set off to meet us yet," says Max.

You hear barking and shouting, and turn back to the ferry. The little dog Trixie is springing along the deck with both a steward and her owner trying to catch her. The steward corners her as she reaches the end of the walkway, but with a leap she jumps onto the hand rail and begins to run along it. The steward makes another grab for Trixie, and the dog loses its footing and tumbles over the side.

Her owner shrieks, and you and everyone else rush to see if they can see the dog in the water. Standing at the rail, you look for any sign of her but can't see her anywhere. Then a short yap draws your attention to a thick rope that is hanging from the rail directly beneath you. Trixie is balanced precariously on the rope! There is no time to lose – you might just reach her if you lean over and hook your leg around the rail.

It is time to make a decision. Do you:

Try to rescue the dog? **P76**

Or

Let the crew deal with the dog? **P9**

8

You have decided to stay with your mother's friend.

Your mother's friend teaches mathematics. As soon as you arrive at her house she gives you a long test.

Then she organizes a three week course in algebra, trigonometry, and calculus. She says you will have a great time, but you wonder if things might have been a little bit more fun if you had chosen to go to Arapawa Island in New Zealand.

It is time to make another decision. Do you:

Change your mind and go to Arapawa Island? **P2**

Or

Stay and do math problems? **P72**

You have decided to let the crew deal with the dog.

The steward hooks his leg over the rail and leans over. He scoops up the dog – which is now very willing to be in his grasp. The steward expertly hoists himself back onto the deck and heads toward the cargo area with Trixie under his arm, and her owner following hurriedly behind.

The ferry finally docks, and huge ropes secure the vessel to the wharf. Tourists and other passengers get ready to go ashore. Most people go down below to their cars. You, Max, and Stella are part of a small crowd to walk off the ship through a gangway that connects with the ferry terminal and land.

A man and a woman have a sign that says 'MAX AND STELLA'.

"Is this Maddy?" you ask Max.

"No," he says, shaking his head. "I don't know who they are."

"Hello!" the man says as the three of you approach. "I'm sorry your aunt Maddy couldn't be here, but we'll look after you. We Islanders take turns getting supplies from the mainland, so we'll take you to the island. Here's a note from your aunt to say it's okay to come with us."

The strangers are called Damon and Sandy. You all walk to their sailboat where you help them finish loading cargo – boxes of food, bags of mail, and big red cans of fuel.

Soon you are all on board and head out into open waters.

10

The waves seem a lot bigger on a smaller vessel! The warm wind smells of the sea. When you are clear of the other boats Damon puts the sails up and cuts the engine. Under sail, the boat cuts smoothly through the water. Without the engine noise you hear the water, gulls, and each other much better.

Dolphins swim ahead of the boat – you grab your camera from your backpack and take some pictures of them leaping out of the water. Damon offers to take a photo of all three of you in the prow of the boat. The beautiful creatures have fun for a while and then disappear to chase a school of fish.

"It's not unusual for dolphins to come up to swimmers and play with them," Sandy said. "You might get a chance to swim with some while you're on the island."

There are not too many boats on this side of the Strait but you see a number of sailboats and fishing boats in the distance. The ferry you travelled on is beginning its home journey. As it passes it sends huge waves towards your boat, which Damon expertly manages. Despite this the smaller boat rocks wildly.

Max points out Arapawa. In front of it are some smaller islands – they are like a pod of dolphins swimming in a group while Arapawa looks like a great whale. To your surprise the boat begins to turn away from Arapawa and toward one of the smaller islands.

"Where are we going?" you ask as the boat slips between two rocky outcrops, and Damon hoists the anchor over the side.

"We're dropping off some supplies at the weather station," explains Damon. "Tell you what – you kids can go up to the station and tell them the supplies are here. Don't take cell phones up there though – the radar will scramble all your data, so you'd best leave them here."

They lower a row boat filled will supplies and help you all climb in. Damon climbs down last of all and rows you all over with a few strong pulls on the oars.

"Just walk straight up the track," he says, pointing up the hill. "I'll unload this gear and get the next lot."

The narrow path slopes upward, and changes from sand to rock, and then dirt and a tangle of tree roots. Just as you are picking your way between the first trees Max turns around and cries out.

You spin around and see that the boat is leaving the little inlet. You all race back down the hill, but the boat is well out to sea. You yell and throw stones to try to get their attention, and then run along the shore trying to keep up with it. Soon, though, it's clear that they are not coming back.

You make your way to the pile of things they have left behind. There are a couple of crates of food and other supplies.

"Is this for us?" Stella says.

Max shakes his head. "It's for the people on the island."

"But why have they left us here?" you ask.

Max crouches to look at the boxes of supplies, and finds a note addressed to himself and Stella:

Don't worry. You will only be here a few days. Take the food up to the hut and stay there.

"If it's a kidnapping, we need to make sure Mum and Dad know we're here before they have to pay a ransom," says Stella.

"Mum and Dad aren't rich," Max says. "Why would anyone want to kidnap us?" He turns to you. "And I don't think they were kidnapping you – they didn't have your name on their sign. I don't think they knew you were coming!"

You are confused too, but try to keep calm and think. "The note says to go up to the hut – let's do that. Maybe there is someone there who can help."

You all pick up the supplies you have been left with and head up the path again.

Now that you have all made a decision to take some action, you start to feel better and have the chance to look around. It is a beautiful place. Birds soar in the sky and flit about in the trees, the sea is blue and the sun feels warm on your face. The path leads you away from the coast, up the hill and into a forest of green trees. It then opens out to a pretty clearing with a cabin in the middle.

It has wooden walls and a metal roof. There is a small porch and one wide step up to it from the grass. You put down the supplies on the porch and see that there is the hook holding the door shut, but it isn't locked. You push it open.

Inside there is one large room with four bunks built against a wall. On the other side are a sink, bench, a stove, and cupboards. In the centre of the room is a wooden table.

There is no sign of anyone.

You go back outside and walk around the hut. There is a large plastic tank with a pipe running to it from the roof, which you figure catches rainwater. There is a smaller shed a short distance away, in amongst the trees, which Max investigates and announces is a 'long drop' – an outdoor toilet.

"We could burn the hut and draw people's attention to rescue us," suggests Max.

"Maybe we should burn the woodpile instead?" you say.

"Maybe we should spend the night here and see if they come and get us in the morning?" says Stella.

It is time to make a decision. Do you:

Burn the woodpile? **P14**

Or

Don't burn the woodpile get ready to stay the night instead? **P27**

You have decided to burn the wood pile.

Burning the wood pile might make smoke that will attract people's attention and get you rescued, so you pile some wood in the clearing well away from the hut, and set it alight with paper and twigs.

At first there isn't much smoke, so you try adding some green branches to the top. It doesn't seem to be working that well, but then you see a bicycle inner tube on the porch. You grab it and drop it on the fire. Thick, smelly smoke starts to pour upwards, as well as a terrible smell of burning rubber.

"I'm going down to the sea again to signal to any boats that come by," you say.

Max and Stella stay behind to mind the fire as you hurry back down the path. Down on the beach you see that the fire isn't very noticeable between the trees. There are no boats in sight.

The plan isn't working, and you head back to the clearing.

Max and Stella are still tending the blaze, but they have done too good a job. Your fire lights some dry leaves and spreads quickly to a pile of dry sticks right beside the water tank. The plastic tank starts to buckle and melt in the heat, and as you watch, water starts pouring out of holes in the tank. The water pours out over the ground and extinguishes the fire with a hiss. Your nose and lungs are filled with the sharp stink of melted plastic. Within a couple of minutes the tank has almost run dry, leaving a pile of wet firewood and a partly melted container.

You feel terrible about destroying the tank. You also realize that there may not be another source of water on the island.

There are only a few more hours of daylight.

It is time to make another decision. Do you:

Explore the island? **P16**

Or

Get ready to stay the night? **P27**

16

You have decided to explore the island.

There is another track heading out of the clearing. The three of you leave your gear at the hut and follow this path. Before long the path becomes very overgrown – nobody has been along here in a long time but you can still make out where it leads.

You crash through weeds – another hundred yards around the hill, you start to hear bees buzzing, and when you round a corner you find an orchard of gnarled old fruit trees sitting in a field of grass. Soon you are all munching on juicy apples.

One tree is much taller than the rest and stands on its own. It's a walnut tree. You climb up into the wide branches hoping to get a better view of the island, and Max climbs up behind you. You can see Arapawa – the island you were supposed to go to. It's infuriatingly close but the rocks, heavy sea, and deep water means there is no way any of you could swim there.

You feel something smooth in the fork of a branch you are holding. You pick it up. It looks like it might be made out of stone, but it's almost white and is very smooth. It's a small carving in the shape of a whale, and you realize that it is made of bone. For a moment you feel like you are losing your balance, and then everything seems fine.

You are just about to share your find with the others when a boy comes into the little orchard. He is carrying a cloth sack and begins to pick apples and put them in his sack. He doesn't see any of you, and as you watch him you put the carving in your pocket.

Before you think to call out to him he sees Stella – then he looks up and sees you and Max. He looks around, perhaps wondering if someone is going to come down from every tree.

"Hi!" says Max. "Did you see our smoke signals?" Your cousin quickly explains that you have been left here and you are trying to get to Arapawa.

"My name's Jack," the boy says. "Sorry, I didn't see the smoke signal at all. I just sailed over from Arapawa Island to get some apples. Do you want me to take you there?"

"That would be great," Stella says. "Can you take us to our aunt Maddy's house?"

"That's odd – I don't know her, but I suppose there are a few people on the island I don't know. If she's there, we can find her."

You are all excited to be rescued and you help him put apples into his sack. You make picking the apples into a bit of a game. One person picks an apple and calls out "Hey!" Then they throw the apple to one of the others. You try to trick each other by looking at one person and throwing to another. Jack is great at it and soon you are all laughing like old friends.

"Come on," Jack says when his sack is full. "We'd better all get going. It's so good you'll be staying on the island – we can come back over here and I can show you some tunnels I found."

You follow him down a path leading to a small cove. Jack's sail boat is very old fashioned and small. There are no life jackets.

He tells you all where he wants you to sit to balance your weight in the water, and then has you help to push the boat out into the water. Jack barks out instructions and expertly maneuvers the boat past rocks – a bigger boat would not have made it into the small harbor.

"I can only go in and out at high tide," Jack says. "There's a cave to explore in the cove as well. That's how I found the tunnels."

When you are between the two islands the wind picks up and some of the waves seem as tall as the boat. You have to yell to be heard over the wind and the splash of the waves, and Jack is too busy to talk much.

Sitting in the boat you start to look at him closely for the first time. He is dressed strangely, in trousers made of a rough grey material and a cotton shirt with wooden buttons that look handmade.

Maybe he is from some alternative, back-to-nature community?

You notice he is wearing a carved necklace – the carving is exactly the same as the one you found at the orchard!

You are about to show him your carving when Jack swings the sail about and you begin to go away from

Arapawa Island – and looking toward the island you can see why. Larger boats are busy in the water ahead and it would have been dangerous to sail among them.

A huge, dark shape suddenly bursts out of the sea between your boat and the big boats. The men in their boats leap into action, running around on deck, frantic with their ropes. A harpoon is launched from the prow of one boat. It arcs up in the air and falls short of the target.

"It's a whale hunt!" Max says.

"We have to do something!" screams Stella. "Those men are hurting the whale – they might kill it!"

Jack looks at her as if she is crazy. "We can't stop them," he says.

"Yes we can!" yells Max. "Put your boat between the whale and the men – they won't shoot us!"

"That's my father's men – if I did that, he'd skin me alive."

Jack shakes his head and looks to you for support.

Something about this isn't right. Surely whaling stopped in these waters years and years ago?

Fortunately, the whale has avoided the hunters – you see its shape leap high into the air and then dive. You hope it is heading far away.

You are getting closer to the shore, now. On the beach there are other boats, and big sheds beyond them. Jack is making ready to land, pointing the boat towards the beach as he lowers the sail and ties off ropes. You see his whale carving again and remember the one you found.

You take it from your pocket and show it silently to Jack. When he sees the whale carving he looks confused and reaches for his own at his throat.

"But that's just like the one I carved," he says.

As he touches his carving you get the same dizzy feeling you felt in the tree earlier. The boat and Jack begin to fade. A moment later you, Max, and Stella are all in the waist-deep water, catching hold of each other and struggling to stand against the waves. The three of you pull yourselves onto the beach – looking back, there is no sign of Jack or his boat.

Standing dripping on the beach, you see that it is now bare – the sheds you saw earlier are gone.

"I think he was a ghost," says Max.

"Then what about the whaling?" Stella asks. "Do you think that was ghosts too? I think we went back in time."

That seems to make sense – or at least, as much as any of this makes sense. You look around to try and figure out where you are and how far from Maddy's little harbor you might be.

You walk a little way up the beach and find the ruins of a small building – did you see this from the boat with Jack?

After a bit of discussion about what to do next you all set off down the beach together, with the warm afternoon sun drying your clothes. After ten minutes you can see a small old house a short way up the hill. There is smoke coming out the chimney.

You find a path through the trees so follow it. As you near the house a large dog rises from the porch and begins to bay. A man comes out of the door, but your excitement at being able to tell someone about your bizarre day turns to terror as you realize he is holding a shotgun!

"This is private property – keep moving!" he yells.

"We need to call the police! We need to use your telephone!" Stella shouts back. The dog leaves the porch and starts to head towards you – a low growl comes from its throat. None of you are keen to go closer.

"I don't have a phone – keep moving! Don't let me catch you on my land again!"

You don't need to be told again, and decide to keep walking in the direction Stella thinks Aunt Maddy lives.

The path that you followed to the house continues on up the hill, so you keep walking up it. Before too long it brings you to the top of the low hill and you walk along, keeping to the top of the hills so you can look down each valley. It's starting to get late in the day and you're feeling tired, but as the sun starts to set you can see her yellow house in the last of the daylight.

You head down, following a rough sheep or goat track and trying not to trip up in the dark. Lights come on in the house as it gradually gets darker. The path ends behind an old shed beside Aunt Maddy's house, and you are about to follow Max and Stella around the corner when they stop in their tracks.

You peer around the side of the shed and see two figures on the porch. It's your kidnappers! You, Stella, and Max all duck back behind the shed and listen.

"Did you hear something?" says a woman – that must be Sandy.

"Sheep – she has them running loose all over." That must be Damon.

There is a slurping sound as one of them sips from a cup, and then Damon speaks again. "Do you think she'll crack?"

"Yeah, she's very close to giving up – now it's dark she'll be really worried about those kids."

"Hope so."

So your kidnapping has something to do with Maddy – but what? You have to get word to her that the three of you are okay so she won't do whatever it is they want her to do. Signaling for Stella and Max to stay where they are, you creep around the back of the house.

The back door is not locked, so you slip inside and stealthily tread down the corridor. The tiniest sound seems so loud and you can hear your own heart like a drum, but you can still hear Damon and Sandy talking outside. In the lounge you see a woman tied to a chair. She is not looking your way so you tap on the door frame. You put a finger to your lips as she looks towards you.

"We are free," you whisper. Then you shrink back into the shadows as Sandy comes back into the room.

"Maddy," Sandy says, "the kids will be safe tonight, but

by tomorrow they are going to get hungry and scared. We have all the time in the world – but they don't. We just want you to sign a paper – it's as simple as that."

"I've told you, Sandy – this process needs to stay with the university. We can't tie it up with one company."

"We are your research partners. This device is as much a part of our work as yours! Why don't you trust us?"

"Trust you?" said Maddy. "You are kidnappers!"

What can you do? In your pockets there is nothing except the bone carving you found on the island, and you rub its smooth surface as you try to think. At that moment there comes a loud crash from the porch, and then growling and barking. Sandy rushes to the door and you leap forward to untie Maddy.

"Hands up where I can see them!" instructs a man's voice outside, and through the open door you can see Sandy comply.

"Maddy, are you in there?" the man shouts.

"Yes! I'm just being untied," she yells back. "Those people are kidnappers and thieves."

In a few moments, Maddy joins her rescuer and together they use the ropes to tie Damon and Sandy back-to-back. It is the angry old man who sent you off his property earlier. Now he is putting his talents to good use!

Before you know it, Stella, Max, and you are munching thick slabs of melted cheese on toasted bread. You were famished! The police have been called and say they will be over in the morning – you will all take turns to watch the criminals until then.

As you sip a hot chocolate, Maddy introduces you all to her gruff neighbor, Jack. Jack was born on the island, and his father and grandfather grew up here too. His family was one of the last to hunt whales in New Zealand.

"I'm glad to say that whaling died with my father," he says. "I'm sorry I was so rude earlier today, kids – I didn't recognize you. But after you left I realized I had met you before."

"No, Jack, I don't think you could have met them before," says Maddy.

"Oh, we didn't meet on this island," you say. "We met on the island we were marooned on. But… it's complicated."

"Now Maddy," says Jack, "why did these stupid people who are tied up on your porch want to tie YOU up?"

Maddy sighs. "For years I've been researching ways to generate power from the tide. It's a natural source of energy with almost no environmental problems. Finally I have some very promising results. My colleagues have been talking to some private companies and they have been offered a lot of money to sell our technology. That's not what I intended. I want this technology to be used by everyone – not patented by a few companies who just want to make lots of money from it instead of giving people cheap electricity."

You and Jack look at each other and smile – you connected across 60 years in one day. Silently, you hand him his carved whale.

"I made this when I was 11 years old," he says.

"The day I took you across in my boat I was so excited I was going to have friends my own age on my island. You showed me your carving just as we were about to land – as I looked at it you all seemed to fade away – I could even sort of see you in the water. My boat landed and all I had was a sack of apples.

"I put the carving in the walnut tree that same summer. I went back often to see if you had reappeared, and when I got older I built the hut there in case you or some other group were marooned there and I wasn't around."

He laughed to himself. "Well guys, welcome to Arapawa. And now we've had the welcome party – what do you want to do with yourselves?"

"I'm thinking of serious sleeping and eating," says Max, and everyone laughs.

"Sounds good to me," says Maddy.

"When you've done with that you'd be welcome to come over to my cove and try some surf casting," says old Jack. "I would take you back to the little island, but I've leased it to a film crew who are doing a project in the caves. They, and one other tenant over there, like their privacy. It's odd you didn't meet them though."

The rest of your time on the island is a blur of land and sea adventures. You are almost eaten by a giant squid, you rescue a sailor, and you explore abandoned homesteads and find a ship wreck. You catch your own fish and, finally, swim with the dolphins!

The End (sort of!)

It is time for another decision. Do you:

Go back to the beginning and try another path? **P1**

Or

Go to the List of Choices and start reading from another place? **P90**

You have decided to get ready to stay the night.

You rummage through the things you have been left. There are only two sleeping bags, but there are some extra blankets. You give the sleeping bags to Max and Stella and offer to use the blankets – as long as you get a top bunk.

Now – food.

There is a little gas stove in the kitchen area and it has a tank of gas, so you unload the supplies and look through everything, trying to decide what you can make for dinner. You combine three ready-made camping meals to make one big pot of macaroni cheese – you're lucky that there is bottled water in with the supplies, or you would be in trouble.

After eating dinner you all sit out on the porch as the rest of the day slips away and the sun sets. Around you birds are settling noisily in the trees, but as it gets dark it becomes quieter again. You can hear the sea lapping against the beach down below.

Max heats up some water to make hot chocolate, and Stella sets up a battery lantern on the table. She hunts around in the supplies and brings out two packets of biscuits.

"Well, we aren't going to starve here," says Max.

"As long as you aren't in charge of the food, that is!" laughs Stella.

You all nibble biscuits and drink your hot chocolate in

silence. Max and Stella both yawn and you realize how tired you are, and soon everyone is wrapped up ready to sleep.

"Should we tell some stories?" Stella asks.

"No offence, you guys, but I'm not in the mood for ghost stories," says Max, and you all agree. It's been a strange day.

You play a game of I Spy, and then you hear Stella climbing out of her sleeping bag.

"I need to go to the toilet," she says. "Max, can you come with me to the long drop?"

He groans, but gets out of his sleeping bag and follows her outside. They take the lamp with them, and Stella carries a roll of toilet paper. Lying in the dark you kind of wish you had a brother or a sister with you for stuff like that. Max and Stella tease each other, but they also look after each other.

A few minutes later, Max and Stella come in laughing. As Max puts down the lamp, Stella accidentally drops the toilet paper and it unravels as it rolls across the floor. It veers off on the uneven floorboards. She follows the paper and bends to pick it up.

"Hey," Stella says. "I think there's a trap door or something here."

"Don't be crazy," says Max.

Together they look at the floor, and sure enough there are lines forming a large square.

"It looks like maybe something fits in here," says Max, pointing at a small metal hole in the wood.

"What do you think would be down there?"

"It's probably just more firewood or something. We should just leave it till morning."

"I want to know what's down there," Stella says. "I won't be able to get a wink of sleep."

All three of you look around the hut for something to use as a lever, and you spy a big metal spoon on the bench. It doesn't fit too well, but you can make the trapdoor lift a little. Stella grabs a spatula, and the next time you try to lift the floorboards she slides it in the gap you've made. Max grabs the edge with his fingers and heaves, and soon the three of you have the trap door open.

Under the trap door there are stairs carved into rock leading down to blackness. The stairs are manmade but the hole looks very old. Someone has cleverly built the hut to disguise this old tunnel entrance. You look at each other, grab the lamp, and head underground. At the bottom of the stairs there is a door with a big, old fashioned lock, and you are surprised to find it's not locked. The door looks a lot older than the hut.

Holding your breath, you silently push at the door – it might be old, but the hinges are well oiled and it opens noiselessly. You can see a corridor sloping downwards. It's made of concrete and rock, and here and there are braces in the ceiling made of wood. It looks like a cross between a mineshaft and a small railway tunnel.

"This place is cool!" whispers Max.

"What if someone's down here?" Stella asks.

You creep forward, and are just about to speak when you realize you can see a light up ahead, around a corner. Stella snaps off the lamp.

Around the bend there is an intersection where the tunnel you are in joins a larger corridor to form a T. Light is coming from a fluorescent tube on the ceiling. It shines in the centre of the intersection where you are standing, making a pool that fades out to black both ways.

It is time to make a decision. Do you:

Turn left? **P31**

Or

Turn right? **P43**

You have decided to turn left.

Turning left, you walk down the tunnel which gradually widens. Here and there you can make out chisel marks in the rock where people have widened the space, but the rest of the rock face seems natural. More lights stud the ceiling and there is a strange noise overhead. It seems incredible that you are walking around inside the island. You realize the noise you can hear is the sea – the tunnel has taken you under the ocean!

You walk on, looking out for any signs of people, and enter a wider antechamber. The first room you come to contains lots of food and other supplies, a lot with strange pictures on the packets and foreign words written on the cans. On a shelf on one side there are chocolate bars and biscuits, and there are large sacks of rice and potatoes. You leave the room and continue exploring.

Now you start to hear another noise – a sort of slow stamping sound. In a room off to one side you can see a machine, and a man standing beside it with his back to you all. The noise of the machine and the sea means he has not heard you. You wonder: Is he friend or foe?

You signal to Max and Stella to stay hidden, then bravely walk up to the man and tap him on the shoulder. He jumps and spins around with an astonished look on his face.

"Who you are?" he gasps. "Is anyone else here with you?"

"No…" you say, sensing he might not be a friendly

person who wants to help. "I'm on my own. I found my way down from the hut. Can I get a lift over to the other island, or use a phone? My aunt will be looking for me."

The man shakes his head. "No phones here. Where's your boat?" You can't really tell what the man's accent is, but you don't think he is a local.

"My boat sank," you say. "I did something really stupid."

The man laughs, but it isn't friendly. "We'll get you sorted – come with me."

He leads you out of the work room and further down the corridor – it suddenly occurs to you that it's still night outside, but the fluorescent lights in this tunnel mean it could be any time of the day. You hope that Max and Stella are following and keeping hidden – you don't dare to look behind you and give them away. The man leads you past a few doors. Some of them are open, and you can see small bedrooms. The tunnel is heading upwards again.

Soon you reach another large room – there is music quietly playing, and in one corner there is a pool table, along with an exercycle and bench for lifting weights. On the other side there is a kitchen and dining area. Two men are eating at the dining table. They watch as you are led past them to a closed door.

The man opens it and leads you though into a sort of office. It has three regular walls, but the last wall is mostly rock with a window set into it. You think that it must look out to the sea when it's daylight. There is a desk on one side of the room, as well as two couches.

"Welcome to my island!" a woman says, and you turn to see her entering the room. She has tousled red hair and is dressed in jeans, sneakers, and a polo-necked sweater.

"Congratulations on making your way into the inner sanctum. I'm Mrs Rogers, but most people around here call me The Director."

"What is this place all about?" you ask.

"The cave system was carved out by the sea. There was once a large blowhole that spouted up through the main cavern – but earthquakes have raised the island and left the chambers dry. This place was first used by the native Maori people as a place to shelter when they were bringing precious greenstone from the South Island to the North."

You have heard of the Maori, the first people of New Zealand. Their descendants still live all over the country today. What they call greenstone is also called jade, and it's worth a lot of money.

"Next," Mrs Rogers explains, "early whalers used these caves to shelter in when the seas got rough. It was nearly forgotten until World War 2 when this place got a major overhaul – it was used by the army to look out for Japanese ships and planes, and after that it was sold into private hands. Today, it is leased to my company."

"And what does your company do?" you ask.

"Before I answer you, how about we invite your friends to join us?"

Stella and Max walk into the room, escorted by a young man with a clipboard. You all sit down on the couches and a plate of toasted bread dripping with honey appears from somewhere, along with another plate with crisp slices of pear and kiwifruit. Mrs Rogers clicks some buttons at her desk and a video begins to run on a screen set in one of the walls. You see pictures of the three of you coming down into the caves!

"We were alerted to your presence on the island when you entered the trap door – you tripped our sensors, and then our cameras followed you. It was a smart move to split up and see what would happen when you approached Hank. You have every reason to be suspicious about people in a strange underground hideaway. We hadn't had time to tell him that we had unexpected guests – so you certainly surprised him!

"This is the setting for a reality TV series. There will be people up above and people down below, and they won't know about each other's existence in the beginning. The people aren't here yet, though."

"I wonder how long they will take to find each other?" says Max.

"Excuse me Mrs Rogers – do you have a boat to get us to Arapawa Island? We think our aunt is worried about us." Stella has said what everyone has been thinking.

"Sure! I will get you over there as soon as we have a camera crew together."

"A camera crew?" you ask.

"Of course! I want you to be part of my reality show. The other thing I'm going to need you to do is to sign non-disclosure contracts – you can't talk about our operation here until we have finished, or it will ruin the show."

"How long will it take to get the film crew together?" you ask.

"No more than two days."

You start thinking that Mrs Rogers isn't being very helpful. Maybe she is more interested in ratings than anything else. Before you can think of what to say she points out that there is no way you could navigate the rocks at night, anyway.

"It's getting late. Let's get you kids to bed!" She points to one of her staff and tells you to follow him.

Mrs Rogers sends you all off to the bedrooms you saw earlier. They are small rooms, perhaps originally used for soldiers. There is a connecting door between your rooms which is unlocked for you. After the assistant leaves, you meet in Max's room.

"There is something weird about all this," says Stella. "I don't think I believe Mrs Rogers."

"I don't either," you say.

"Me neither," says Max, "but it's too dark to take a boat over to the island now, so there's no point trying to escape yet. In the morning we should scout around for one and try to escape."

You all agree – but you wonder if a bit of scouting later tonight might be useful too.

You climb up into your bunk and find yourself falling asleep almost instantly. In the middle of the night you wake and wonder where you are, and then the whole drama comes flooding back. While it makes sense to wait till morning to leave the island, it doesn't make sense to wait a few days. Your parents and Aunt Maddy will be worried. Maybe there is something else that Mrs Rogers is trying to hide.

You decide to have another look at the room where you met the first of her assistants. You slowly slip out of your bunk and pull on your clothes.

Remembering the cameras in the corridor, you don't switch on any lights and instead decide to feel your way. You leave a sneaker outside your door so you will know which one is your room when you return. Then, you start creeping up the tunnel – you can tell you are moving in the right direction because the ground is sloping upwards. You run your hand along the wall to feel the doors – one, two, three, this next one might be it…

As you start opening the door you hear snoring – you must have counted wrongly, and this is another bedroom! You quietly shut the door again and keep going up the corridor. You stop at the next door – okay, THIS must be it.

You listen carefully before stepping inside and closing the door softly behind you. It takes a moment to find the light switch. It's so bright after the pitch black that you have to squint. Your heart thumps, but nobody comes. You cross the room and look at the machinery, trying to work out what it is or what does. Then it hits you – it's a printing press, and stacked to one side you see money, lots of it, all in $100 bills! There is Australian currency, New Zealand currency, and others. These people aren't making a TV show – they're forgers!

There are some empty plastic bags on the bench. You slip a variety of the fake money into one of the bags and cross back to the door. Just in time, you remember to switch off the light before opening the door. You feel for the knob and then slip back out in the corridor.

Feeling your way back towards your room, you are relieved when your toe finds the sneaker you left outside. You clamber back into bed, and sleep.

You are awoken hours later by Stella and Max. In moments you are up and ready too, with the money stashed in your pocket. You sneak through the big open-plan room with the kitchen, and luckily there is nobody around. You go through a door in the direction you think might lead to the sea, and maybe a boat. Sure enough, you find yourself outside on a ledge which slopes down to the sea – in the early dawn light you can see that there are three motor boats moored there.

Max and Stella have been in boats before and have an idea how they work, so Max sits in the driver's seat while

Stella casts off. She jumps in when Max starts the boat and looks over the controls.

"It's like a dirt bike on water," he declares.

As the boat begins to move forward, you hear a shout from behind you. It's one of the assistants, waving his arms for you to stop.

"Come back! You'll kill yourselves!"

It is time to make a decision. Do you:

Listen to the assistant and stop? **P73**

Or

Escape in the boat? **P39**

You have decided to escape in the boat.

Max gives the boat a burst of power and it surges out
through a small rocky channel. On the console, a screen
comes to life showing the terrain underneath the boat – you
can see an outline of the bottom of the boat, and not far
below it are rocks!

"Stella, watch the screen for rocks underneath us," says
Max as he steers and you both help him navigate out to sea.

As you leave the channel the sea level drops off sharply
and you no longer have to worry about rocks. In fact, you
can make out the shapes of fish beneath you. Some of them
are very big.

Looking back, it is already hard to see where you came
from – the cove is well hidden. You are now in open water
and Max points the boat toward the island you should be on
– Arapawa. It is very close.

Stella is no longer glued to the depth finder screen, but as
she straightens up she shouts, "Oh no!"

You turn to see that another boat is emerging from the
hidden cove. There are three figures on board, and one of
them has red hair blowing in the wind – Mrs Rogers. Her
boat picks up more speed as soon as it is past the rocks and
starts to close the gap between you.

"We have to speed up!" you yell at Max.

He pulls on the throttle and the boat leaps forward. Out
here the waves are bigger, and the increased speed makes the

boat seem very unstable. Arapawa Island is getting closer – you are more than half way there – and you hope you will get to the island before Mrs Rogers catches up. The boat she is on is bigger, and you worry she might ram you.

The beach is in sight now, and Max is just heading straight for it rather than the little jetty.

Suddenly, Stella grabs the wheel and pulls it to one side – the depth finder is showing rocks beneath you again, and Stella has just avoided some big ones!

Looking back, you can see a large wave coming up behind Mrs Rogers' boat – they are now close enough that you can see their angry faces. The wave picks them up, and then it carries your boat too. It's like being on a surf board, and Max increases speed to take advantage of it.

In moments you are beached on the golden sand, and scramble out of the boat on to dry land. Behind you Mrs Rogers' boat is still in the sea…. and it isn't moving. The wave has wedged it on the rocks that Stella avoided.

Mrs Rogers doesn't look as scary wedged precariously on the rocks, but she does look as angry as a hornet. A voice suddenly speaks up from behind you.

"Don't worry, the boat will come loose at high tide and the police can get them off. Who are those people?"

A friendly looking woman has joined you on the beach. Stella and Max throw themselves onto her – it's Aunt Maddy. Maddy explains that your 'kidnappers' had left you on the little island to try and press her into selling her rights to the little harbor – they want to set up a business there. Maddy didn't stand for blackmail, though – she threatened to call the police straight away.

"So Damon went over to the island to get you and then came back to say you had disappeared! So then I *did* call the police, and they have been looking for you too. Oh, here they are now!"

A powerful police launch has come into view and sweeps into the little harbor. They see Mrs Rogers in trouble and throw a rope over to her boat. The police drag the smaller vessel off the rocks and in no time Mrs Rogers is on shore beside you.

She is busy explaining to the police that she is part of a reality TV show when you remember the plastic bag you are carrying. You hand it to one of the officers.

"Mrs Rogers might be making a TV show," you say, "but they are also busy making these."

The policeman looks into the bag and his eyes widen in surprise. The scene quickly changes – Mrs Rogers stops explaining about her TV show, and is instead arrested and taken away on the police launch.

"Well," says Aunt Maddy, "after all that excitement I think you'll want some breakfast and to get started on your proper holiday?"

"Yes!" you all agree. Then you set off up to the house. It's been a great start to your holiday but you wonder what if you'd made some different choices?

It is time to make a decision. Do you:

Start the story over and make different decisions? **P1**

Or

Go to the list of choices and pick another place to start reading? **P90**

You have decided to turn right.

Turning right, you head down a sloping tunnel. The walls are roughly hewn as if people have widened an existing schism in the rock. There are large spider webs across the roof and sides of this section of the tunnel, like a giant spider has made this its nest. Max shudders as he brushes against one of the cobwebs, but Stella, unafraid, puts her hand out to pull it off him.

"Not much for spiders to catch down here," she says. "Hmmm... they're fake!"

In a few minutes you begin to hear old fashioned music. You can see light around the next door you come to. It's locked, so you all bang on it to be heard over the music. The song finishes abruptly and the door opens.

The man who is standing in the doorway is much older than the pictures you've seen, but you still recognize him, and when he speaks you know his voice.

Max blurts out, "But... you're dead!"

"Well, Max – my career is dead, but I'm alive and well."

He lives in a fabulous cave that makes you think of the inside of a genie's bottle. The cave walls are covered in richly colored fabrics, and Oriental rugs cover the floor. Peering in, you see that beyond the main room is a full kitchen, and you can see a room through a window that looks like it might be a recording studio. The old rock star smiles at your curiosity and beckons you in. In the kitchen he makes you all a hot chocolate. He tells you how his fame got too much for him, and when he realized he had enough money he organized his 'exit'.

"It got so I couldn't enjoy my life at all. I was followed everywhere – so I decided to disappear."

"Hey," says Stella. "How come you knew my brother's name when we met you?"

"Well spotted, Stella! That's because you've been down here already tonight. We talked and I explained about my private life, and then you kindly let me hypnotize you so you would forget our meeting. It worked, but unfortunately you made the same choice to come back this way. If you don't mind, I'll do it again and try to put in a stronger suggestion that you go another direction. I hope you understand?"

"Okay," says Max, "but only if I can jam one tune with the King."

The older man laughs and tells you and Stella to stand by to sing the backup vocals – again!

Five minutes later after the excitement of singing, he lines you, Max, and Stella up by the door and says, "You are feeling sleepy…"

The next time you open your eyes, you are at the fork of a tunnel.

Now you have to make a decision Do you:

Turn left? **P31**

Or

Turn right? **P43**

You've finally decided to go to Arapawa Island.

The island of Arapawa is large – Maddy explains there are only a few people spread over the island. Maddy has her own harbor in a horseshoe-shaped bay with another little island in its centre. Her boat, the *Seahorse*, is moored in the bay. Maddy explains that her land reaches up to the top of the hills that create the valley, and it is covered in a mixture of green subtropical forest and pasture. You look up at the hills and can see sheep and some goats.

Maddy lives in an old fashioned farm house with a full front veranda. A fenced garden surrounds the veranda – it's a wild mixture of herbs, flowers, and vegetables.

There are solar panels on the roof and several small wind turbines sit on fence posts around the house.

"I'm pretty much self-sufficient," she says, "which is important because in bad weather the island can be cut off from the mainland for days. Come on, let me show you your digs."

Halfway up the hill behind the house is a large shed with a bunk house attached.

"This land used to be part of a large sheep farm. Each year a shearing gang would come from the mainland and stay here while they sheared the wool from the sheep. Nowadays I let writers and scientists use it for a place to do some thinking. Why don't you kids settle in, and then come round to the house before dark."

You wander through the bunk house. The walls are all whitewashed and the floors are bare boards made smooth by all the feet that have travelled over them. There is a small central kitchen and living area. Several old armchairs circle a big stone fireplace. Beside it is a bookshelf, so you have a look at the books. You see a history of whaling in New Zealand, a couple of cookery books, a few thrillers and mysteries, books about fishing and sailing, and a semaphore manual. There are cards and old fashioned dice and word games. You wonder what it would be like to live here all the time.

"This is my room!" shouts Stella.

You hurry to find your own bunk. There are four doors off from the main living area. Stella has called out from one. You hear Max rustling about from another. Through another door you can see a short corridor that leads to the bathrooms. That leaves one more door – you open it and see a narrow flight of stairs. When you reach the top you see you are on the level above the living area – there is a table and a bed. Stella and Max come up to find you.

"Awesome," says Max, looking at your attic space.

You all grab your bags and drag your gear to your rooms.

Just then there is a clanging sound from outside – you head to the big house. Aunt Maddy is there ringing an old bell.

"This bell was here when my family bought the house when I was your age. My mother used to ring it to bring me back home for dinner – now I'm the one ringing the bell."

The smell of fresh bread draws you all inside. On the table sits a roast chicken, potatoes, gravy, and asparagus and green beans. There is a pile of bread rolls and a huge tossed salad. Soon you all have full plates. Later, when you are all full, Maddy tells you to take the leftovers back to the shearing shed's little kitchen.

"There should be plenty for sandwiches for lunch tomorrow – you can take them exploring or go fishing and see if you can catch yourselves tomorrow night's meal. I've left you things for breakfast, so if you don't need me you can just do your own thing till dinner."

Clearly, Aunt Maddy hasn't had children of her own and doesn't seem to be worried that you will come to any harm.

That night you lie in bed and listen to the quiet noises of the island. A sheep or a goat bleats somewhere, there is the quiet constant lapping of the water, and you can hear an owl somewhere in the trees.

The next day you wake up to the smell of toast. In the kitchen you find Max cheerfully smearing butter and honey onto a stack of thick browned slices of bread. Stella staggers into the room, rubbing her eyes.

Through the window, the sea glistens under a bright blue sky. You all take your breakfast outside onto the porch. Sitting on the steps you can see the sea fade from green just below you to blue out by the horizon. As you sit in the sun and bite into grainy goodness a small goat makes its way up the path and comes up to you. It bleats a greeting and then quickly takes the toast from your hand! It looks at you as if it does this every morning and can't work out why you look so surprised, and then trots back toward the hills. Oh well, there is plenty more toast.

You all pack some lunch into your backpacks and grab your fishing rods. You see Stella has a book – good idea. You randomly grab a book off the shelf and see it is the semaphore book that you are stuffing into your bag's side pocket.

You head down to the shore.

"What shall we do," says Max. "Shall we fish or go exploring?"

It is time to make a decision. Do you:

Go fishing? **P49**

Or

Go exploring? **P56**

You have decided to go fishing.

You head down to the sandy bay you arrived at yesterday. You walk along the beach and then clamber up into the forest to find a natural path to follow around the coastline and away from the shelter of the bay. The waves lap gently down below you, but as the shore turns rocky the water begins to surge and slap.

You pick your way down to where the rocks sit just above the water. Close to the water's edge, rock pools hold multicolored anemones and little fish. The pools are like little cities – busy with life.

The fish dart away when your shadow falls over them, and you feel like a giant. Stella puts her fingers into the water. She lightly touches an anemone and it clamps shut like an alien eye.

A small fish would be trapped and digested in its grip. You are impressed by these beautiful little monsters. Stella gets out her camera and tries to get a picture of the life inside the rock pool.

"This would make a good app," she says. "It would be cool to manage your own rock pool."

"Come on!" Max shouts from a rocky ledge just above you.

You and Stella follow him up some natural steps. Striped limpets stud the cliff and there are little pockets of water in the rock, showing that the tide can reach this far.

"We'll have to watch out for rogue waves here – one big one and we'll be plucked off the rocks," says Max.

You find a wide ledge overlooking the sea and peer over the edge. It's about five yards down to where the waves break against the rock.

You noticed this morning that you don't have any cell phone coverage on the island, so you sit down on the edge and pull the semaphore book out of your bag. Leafing through, you think about how people used to communicate. Stella and Max look over your shoulder.

The book explains how to use one or two flags to represent the alphabet. You don't have flags, but you can use your arms. Before long you are spelling messages to each other and planning how you might be able to signal to each other from greater distances.

After a while you remember that you are meant to be fishing so the three of you bait hooks and then cast your lines. The reels whirr as baited hooks fly and then plop into the sea. Within minutes there is a tug on your line and you begin to reel it back in. As you pull the fish in from the water Max gives a shout and starts reeling in too. A moment later and Stella is also pulling in a fish. Soon there are three silver fish in your bucket.

"They're blue cod," Stella says. "They are great to eat."

"Let's climb up the cliff face and see if we can find some birds' nests," says Max.

"That's a good way to get yourself killed," says Stella. "I

want to catch another fish for Maddy."

It is time to make a decision. Do you:

Climb up the cliff? **P52**

Or

Head back with your fish? **P54**

You have decided to climb up the cliff.

With the bucket of fish tied beneath your backpack you feel for hand and foot holds, and slowly make your way up the cliff. You catch up with Max and look up. Way above you, at the top of the cliff, is a wire fence. Maybe there is a sheep paddock and a different route back. You hope so, because you don't want to have to climb back down this way.

Shrill squawking interrupts your thoughts. A baby seagull sits inside a nest of grass and seaweed. It seems to think you might have come to feed him. Another noise brings your attention back to your climb.

A large seagull is squawking at Max and swooping so close to him that it looks like it will hit Max in the head! Ouch! It feels like stones are hitting the back of your head – another bird is attacking you!

It is almost impossible to shelter your head, but you tuck your face in against the cliff. The gull lands on the bucket swinging beneath you. It's after the fish!

As the bird propels itself skyward with a fish in its bill, it pushes the bucket behind your knees, your legs give way, and you hang for a moment from your hands.

You see the bird flying away triumphantly with a fish as you plummet to the rocks far below.

Arghhhhhhhhhhhhhhhhhhhhhhhhhhh!

Oops, that didn't end very well, did it?. But what would

have happened if you'd made different choices?

It is time to make a decision. Do you:

Go to the beginning and try another path? **P1**

Or

Go to the List of Choices and start reading from another place? **P90**

You have decided to head back with your fish.

You head back toward the shearers' quarters and find Maddy on her front porch, writing at a table. She waves as you approach and takes you in to her kitchen to show you how to clean the fish. She has a trench outside in her garden for the fish guts – it is an ingenious system. She digs in compost and fishing leftovers and then covers it all with dirt. Later she plants a row of giant sunflowers at the edge of her porch have benefited from the smelly plant food.

She shows you where you can dig up new potatoes and carrots, and there are tomatoes growing on a vine. You have never been surrounded by so much food outside a supermarket.

Back in the kitchen, Maddie shows you how to breadcrumb the fish ready for tonight's meal. You tell her about practicing from the semaphore book as she puts the finished fish into the fridge.

"That old book! I used to have some flags so that I could signal to a friend on the mainland. We had great fun sending messages to each other – we found if we dropped out all the vowels in our messages we could communicate much faster.

"Um – that's called text messaging, Auntie," says Stella.

The phone rings and Maddy is still laughing when she picks it up. It's Stella and Max's parents. While you finish tidying up in the kitchen, Stella tells them about your journey here and the shearers' quarters you are staying in.

Max tells his parents about fishing.

You wonder what it must have been like to live on the island before telephones and boats with motors. You head back to the shearers' quarters and lie down on your bed with the semaphore book.

After a while Max comes back, and then Stella.

"What do you want to do?" Stella asks. "Do you want to go swimming or exploring?"

It is time to make a decision. Do you

Go swimming? **P74**

Or

Go exploring? **P56**

You have decided to go exploring.

Up the valley the smell of salt air and the sound of lapping water is replaced by bleating lambs and the occasional clatter of small rocks disturbed by a goat high on the cliff. You agree to go up the hill different ways and then walk along the ridge to meet at the top. The sun is at your back as the three of you climb up the valley.

Max goes to one side, Stella to the other, and you take the middle track which ought to be the shortest way up. You are thinking about the semaphore book – when you get to the top you might signal to the others. You stop and leaf through the book, thinking about a funny message you could make. After a while you realize you had better get moving or you will be last to the top.

You watch the ground as the path becomes much steeper. Pasture turns to bare rock that sparkles here and there with quartz. One section looks like a natural armchair – you sit in it and the stone feels warm from the sun. Over to the left you can see Stella climbing just below a small group of goats. Whenever she gets close the goats move away, but one young kid seems very curious and is slowly letting Stella get closer. You can see that Stella has noticed as well. She reaches into her back pack, takes something out, and throws it toward the kid. The kid comes closer to see what it is. Stella is making a friend.

You reach into your pack and pull out your camera, find

Stella through the viewfinder, and zoom in across the valley as she charms the young goat. You take a few shots as it gets closer and closer and then finally scampers away. Perhaps you can find Max on the opposite side of the valley. Without taking your eye from the camera you swoop down toward your feet and fiddle with the zoom so you can have a wider look for Max.

As your gaze slowly sweeps the ground, a large rock seems to move – zooming in, you find that you are staring at a dinosaur!

You panic, drop the camera and scuttle backwards. Where is it?

With relief, you see it sitting on a rock a few yards away and realize that your dinosaur is a lot smaller when you aren't looking through your camera. No wonder you didn't see it when you sat down – it is almost the same color as the rock, and covered in craggy skin.

Could it bite you? It might be small but you know there are small snakes in the world than can kill with one bite. Meanwhile, your dinosaur hasn't moved – it's just staring up at you. How curious it is – it's quite different to the little geckos and lizards you have seen before. It's like a miniature dragon without the wings.

Glancing to the left, you see that Stella is nearly at the top of the valley, and to the right Max is already walking across the crest of the hill, making his way to your meeting place. Stella is spelling out something in semaphore with her arms:

58

H
U
R
R
Y
U
P

You grab your pack and get moving, thinking of the story you have to tell about meeting a dinosaur.

Before long you make the top of the hill. Stella is telling her brother about her goat. From this height the three of you are able to see much more of the island – from where you stand you can see there is a spine to the island, with a goat track stretching as far as you can see. On each side of the island are valleys like the one you just climbed. You can't see too far into them but the one closest has lots of different trees. The next valley has a longer, gentler slope to the sea. You can see a house and some sheds down toward one of the bays, but closer to you, between the trees, you can spy a very old house and some dilapidated buildings. The trees catch Stella's attention.

"I think those are plum trees! Let's check them out."

Worried that you may be trespassing, you hang back a bit as you climb through brambles and low bushes. It's clear not many people come through this way. As you get closer to the house it's also clear that nobody could live there – there are trees pushing their way up through the old back porch, many of the windows are missing, and the rusted roof is sagging.

It is time to make a decision. Do you:

Go in. **P60**

Or

Don't go in. Go check out the plum trees instead? **P62**

You have decided to go in to the run down house.

The old house is too intriguing to ignore. You gingerly make your way up to it. The boards of the porch creak as you approach the door – it's very slightly open, and it groans as you push it the rest of the way.

You step into the kitchen first. It is warm and musty. The window is covered by a vine which gives the room a green hue as the light travels inside. The floor is covered in old bird droppings and there is a large iron oven, a small table, and two chairs – the chairs are pulled out as if the owners had just decided to leave, stood up, and walked out without packing or looking back. The oven door is ajar and full of bits of grass and branches twisted into a birds nest.

The door to the next room is closed and for a moment you think it might be locked, but with a bit of wriggling the rusted handle moves and you find yourself in a hallway with a strip of moth-eaten carpet running down the middle. Light struggles through the grimy windows of the front door.

You follow the hallway all the way down. You turn to look in the room on the left by the front door, while Max and Stella go to the right. Two large armchairs sit against one wall in your room, and their upholstery looks fragile – a mouse peeps out of a hole and you crouch to look at it. Stella and Max enter the room behind you and you realize you are all keeping very quiet. You are just about to point out the mouse when you hear the ominous creak of the back door.

You look at each other – Stella and Max look as scared as you feel. Maybe it's the wind? Suddenly you hear banging and crashing in the kitchen. All three of you scramble toward the window but as you wriggle the catch the whole frame falls out with a huge bang. The three of you leap out of the hole in the wall and help each other jump down from the front porch. You run into the long grass that might once have been a lawn and hit a solid wall of overgrown trees and bushes. You turn and make your way round the house to the path you made when you came in.

You crouch down as you near the back door and now you hear it – bleating. Stella laughs and heads back to the house and you follow, just in time to see the young goat she fed earlier emerge from the kitchen door, wearing the bird's nest from the oven on its head.

You shoo the goat away and shut the door, not wanting to cause any more damage to the old place.

What should you do next?

It is time to make a decision. Do you:

Go look at the plum tree? **P62**

Or

Go back for a swim? **P74**

You have decided to look at the plum tree.

The plum trees have formed a tight forest around the side of the old house. It reminds you of the fairy tale Sleeping Beauty.

The air is perfumed by the soft sweet smell of ripe plums. You pick one and bring it to your mouth. The dark red fruit is a juicy explosion of sweet and sour in your mouth, and the three of you wander from tree to tree finding the next perfect treat.

"There's a path here!" Max points to a line of trampled grass leading away from the trees.

The three of you wander down the narrow path with a wall of long grass on each side of you. As you turn a bend you find a little shed – it's not as dilapidated as the house, but it's certainly old. As you stand there you are startled by a figure at the door of the shed.

As he moves into the light you see it is a boy a bit older than you. He smiles shyly and says "Hello" in a strong accent. Before you can answer, he asks, "Do you have anything to eat?"

Stella reaches in her backpack and offers her sandwiches to the stranger. He smiles broadly. You all sit down and share your food with him.

"My name is Mikhal," he says. "I swam to shore one night from a fishing boat. My mother and father owed money and when they couldn't pay it, the man took me to work on the boat. I worked on the boat for a miserable year and then knew I had to escape. The debt must have been paid. When I saw land I packed my belongings in plastic and used an old polystyrene box to help me swim to shore."

He sighs, and looks sad. "I want to find job and get the money to go home to my family."

"We can help," you tell him.

As the four of you leave the glade, you ask him where the other path leads.

"It goes to the sea – I looked, but I see lights and think it might be ghosts or fishermen coming to find me. I walk across hills and find I am on island! I sleep here and try to think of plan."

You take Mikhal back to Maddy's house – on the way back you tell the others how you saw a little dinosaur. Stella and Max laugh at you but Mikhal looks serious.

"I know about such things. My captain collects little animals and birds for people. It was my job on the boat to look after the animals – I grew up on a farm and the captain thought I would know what to do. The night I escaped, the fishing boat was close to land because the crew were picking up more animals."

Maddy's house is in sight and Mikhal becomes quiet. He seems nervous about meeting her.

Maddy is in the kitchen when you arrive – you all explain in a rush about finding the castaway. Maddy shakes Mikhal's hand and shows him a spare room where he can put his things. Maddy says she has heard about people exploiting child labor and says that there are laws against it.

"You'll stay here the night, Mikhal. I need to call the police," she tells him. "They will be able to send you home to your family."

Then she finds him a towel and sends him off for a shower and sets the three of you to work readying dinner. She has you busy frying the fish you caught this morning, while Max is cooking vegetables and Stella is cutting up lemons and setting the table. When it is all ready Maddy brings out a large potato salad.

Just then Mikhal arrives from the shower wearing some of Max's clothes. In fact Max and Mikhal are not too different in size, although a year at sea has built Mikhal's muscles. Everyone eats and Mikhal asks the name of everything on the table in English.

When Maddy asks what else you have been up to today you tell her about Stella making friends with a goat. Stella laughs and says at least her friend wasn't imaginary.

Suddenly, you realize that you must have left your camera on the hillside where you saw the little dinosaur.

It is time to make a decision. Do you:

Go outside in the dark to find your camera? **P66**

Or

Stay inside? **P65**

You have decided to stay inside.

You sit down to a game of cards and Maddy teaches you the rules. It doesn't take long to learn the game and then you are all hooked. After a couple of hours, Maddy shoos you off to your own house – Mikhal is looking very tired and you realize that with little food and sleep for the past few days he must be exhausted.

Back in the shearers' quarters, Max and Stella call out to each other for a while before their voices go quiet and you slip off to sleep. In the morning you will all travel to the mainland to take Mikhal to the police and to sort out a plan to get him home.

Before you leave the next morning, you run up the hill to find your camera but find that morning dew has interfered with the memory card, and there are no pictures. You have an enjoyable holiday but you often get the feeling that if you had gone to get your camera that night you might have made an important discovery.

Congratulations, you have reached the end of this part of the story. But have you tried all the possible paths?

It is time to make another decision. Do you:

Go back to the beginning of this story and try another path? **P1**

Or

Go to the list of choices? **P90**

You have decided to go and look for your camera.

The stars seem much brighter than in the city, and there are so much more of them. The moon is almost full and it is like a giant white plate in the sky. You have only taken a few steps up the hill when you hear a shout as Mikhal runs up to join you. Soon you are both striding up the hill. In contrast to this afternoon you are moving fast, but you can't see any animals on the hillside.

"Look up there – Southern Cross." Mikhal is pointing at the stars where they form a shape like a kite. "Old sailors would find their way by the stars."

Soon you come to the place where you dropped the camera and saw the little dinosaur. You and Mikhal stand and wait for the moon to come out from behind a cloud. When it does, you are able to make out a gleam on the ground. The camera! You switch it on and flick through the pictures you have taken. The last picture must have been taken just before you dropped the camera– there is a picture of the rock and the dinosaur! You are so excited you almost drop the camera again.

You show the picture to Mikhal, and he smiles.

"But this is my little dragon! You saw it here? Good, she is alive. I brought her with me when I came ashore."

You start back to the house wondering what Mikhal is talking about. Before the two of you have made it halfway back down the hill, three figures step out of the dark. You jump back in surprise, and Mikhal grabs you by the arm and tries to run, but the men have the advantage. Someone wraps his arms around you and presses a rag over your face. It has a strong smell and you feel yourself blacking out. You fight to stay awake, but it's useless. The darkness comes rushing towards you as you feel yourself being lifted up…

… You come to your senses wondering where you are. There is a rocking motion, and the smell of diesel and seawater. You look around and realize that you are on a bunk in a boat, and you can hear voices outside speaking in a language you can't understand. There is the clink of spoons in coffee mugs, and laughter.

Then the cabin door opens and Mikhal enters. He looks scared and pale, and there is a bruise on one side of his face.

"Oh my friend. The sailors have caught me and they have caught you, too. They are angry I ran away, and they are so angry I have lost their little dragon. It is worth money and now they say we both must work to earn the money back. I am so sorry. I will help you and teach you and then they will not treat you so bad."

You can't believe this is happening – kidnapped! Just then a large man enters the cabin and speaks to Mikhal in the language you don't understand.

"Mikhal," you say. "Tell him to let us go. The police will be looking for us."

The man laughs, and Mikhal translates his words.

"Nobody looks for you! Now you have a job with us

fishing. And if you do not work then you feed the fish! You understand?"

You understand.

You get up and follow Mikhal outside to find that it is bright daylight – you must have slept right through the night. Outside on deck you stagger as the ship moves, and you see that you are well out to sea – there is no land on the horizon, and you couldn't possibly swim ashore.

It is the start of a long, hard day. With Mikhal showing you how, you clean a huge hold that will contain the next haul of fish. From time to time a siren sounds that alerts you to meal breaks, and together you make your way to a mess hall where you are fed alongside ten men – one of these is Mikhal's friend Stan, who taught him English.

As the days pass you get into a routine, and when there is not much to do Stan sits you both down and teaches you something. You never know what the lesson might be, but it becomes your main source of new information and entertainment.

Another of your duties is to take care of the animals. The captain has a collection of birds and lizards in various cages. You and Mikhal clean the cages and make sure each animal has water and fresh food. In a large glass container you find several more of the little dinosaurs, or dragons, as Mikhal calls them. These are the creatures that caused you so much trouble. Something about them keeps nagging at your memory, but you don't know what it is.

The animals are kept deep in the ship, through a hidden door next to the engines. It's loud in there and you think the birds mustn't like it very much. Some of them are beginning to pull out their feathers, and they look a bit downcast.

The ship is like a factory with processing and freezing facilities. Several times you try to get to the captain's office where instruments and presumably a radio are kept, but each time you are blocked from entering by the crew. Eventually, when nobody is around, you get closer but find that the doors have keypad locks, and you don't know the code. You are a prisoner, but as long as you work you are fed.

The days are getting warmer and you know you have been heading north for a week now. The holds are full of fish and it seems that the ship has completed its work and is heading to offload its cargo.

On the twelfth day of your kidnapping, you see land in the distance. The ship gradually gets closer, and just as you are planning to jump overboard a burly sailor grabs you and locks you and Mikhal in the animal room. You stay there for two days – from time to time you are sent food, but no matter how hard you bang on the door nobody comes to let you out until you are out to sea again.

The next morning you and Mikhal are washing down the foredeck when a yacht comes into view. Not wanting to draw attention from the crew, you both move so that you are mopping behind one of the ship's funnels. Calmly, you perform the semaphore signals you learnt on the island, repeating the same message over and over until one of the crew notices what you are doing and locks you below. You hardly dare hope that someone on the yacht saw your message. Even if they did – would they know what it meant?

The next day you are back on deck when you hear a helicopter. You and Mikhal are quickly hustled below deck to the room where the animals are kept. You are there for hours before the door is opened by an Australian naval officer. You can't hear what he is saying over the noise of the engine, but you can see his surprise as he looks at the cages. He signals for both of you to follow him out.

Above deck you find that the crew has been rounded up. A large naval ship is alongside the fishing boat, and there are men and women in navy uniforms everywhere. You and Mikhail are swung across to the bigger ship, and soon you are telling your story to the authorities.

The Australian officers tell you that the yacht you signaled to had a retired naval officer aboard – he could read your semaphore message and called the navy. You and Mikhal can be returned to your parents or back to the island – you have saved a number of rare birds, and the little dragons are rare New Zealand tuatara that were stolen from a wildlife sanctuary.

The day after you were kidnapped, Max and Stella found your camera and the picture you had taken of the tuatara. Everyone realized that your disappearance might be linked to the missing lizards, and the New Zealand and Australian navy have been looking for you. If the greedy captain hadn't kidnapped you then the tuatara and other endangered creatures would have been lost to private collectors, and could have become extinct in the wild.

You are returned home and Mikhal goes home to his parents. Months later you hear that you have both come into possession of the fishing boat as reparation for your kidnapping and forced labor.

The two of you set up a trust, and the boat is renamed *Tuatara*. It becomes a conservation vessel, travelling the Pacific Ocean helping marine biologists save endangered species.

Congratulations, you've reached the end of this part of the story.

That means it is time to make another decision. Do you:

Go back to the beginning of this story and try another path? **P1**

Or

Go to the list of choices and start reading from a different part of the story? **P90**

You have decided to stay and do math problems.

Question One:

A New Zealand giant squid can drag someone your weight and strength down to the bottom of a three mile trench in ten minutes. How many minutes would it take for two giant squid to drag you down to a watery grave?

Question Two:

You find a device which moves you backwards and forwards in time. You find out that you move back one hundred years every time you hit the back button and you move forward fifty years every time you hit the forward button. You travel back 300 years and find yourself being chased by a giant eagle. The Haast's eagle was the largest eagle ever known to have lived and has been extinct for two hundred years. How many times do you have to hit the forward button to avoid being a meal for a giant eagle?

Question Three:

While Lost in Lion Country you find yourself left alone with the safari picnic basket. There are 50 ham sandwiches inside the basket. One hyena will be satisfied after 10 ham sandwiches and will head off to sleep in the sun. How many hyena can you hold off until help arrives?

(For answers **P92**)

You have decided to stop.

Seeing you hesitate, the agile assistants swarm onto the boat and pull you back to shore. You are frog-marched to the main room inside, and as one of the men goes to find Mrs Rogers the bag of money that you took falls out of your pocket.

"Look," shouts one of the men as he snatches it up, "they know everything!"

Mrs Rogers strides into the room. "Okay, kids – this is going to be a working holiday. I tried to come up with a way you could go home to mummy and daddy, but you had to ruin it by sneaking into things that don't concern you. Well now you'll work. For the next four weeks you can learn how to make money – and when we're done here we'll drop you off somewhere and you can make your way back to civilization. Behave, or you'll be fish food!"

She bundles you into the printing room. For the next month you work day and night, making fake money and hoping each day won't be your last…

You have reached the end of this part of the story. But have you tried all the possible paths?

It is time to make a decision. Do you:

Go back to the beginning and try another path? **P1**

Or

Go to the list of choices? **P90**

You have decided to go for a swim.

It's a hot day and the lapping of salt water on your toes is delicious. The sand beneath the waters has been warmed by the sun and feels like chocolate pudding between your toes as you wade deeper in.

Max and Stella are kitting up with snorkels and masks. You dive under a wave and swim out into the bay. The three of you move out deeper and deeper. Max and Stella dive under and when they come back up they tell you about fish they see.

They muck about flicking seaweed at each other. Suddenly the water feels a lot colder.

"That's because it's so much deeper now – it's about two miles deep out here," says Stella.

They dive back down again, and then you feel one of them tickling your leg – it almost feels like a snake. Stella surfaces a few feet away and Max on the other side – they are yelling and waving. Hang on – what is grabbing your leg, then?

The snaking feeling becomes stronger. A huge tentacle writhes up out of the water and then turns towards you and clamps onto your arm. It is a giant squid. The last thing you think as you are dragged below is how incredibly rare a death like this must be — glub, glub, glub.

Well that's the end of this part of your story. What a way

to go! Good thing this is a 'you say which way' adventure, because you can start over.

It is time for you to make another decision. Do you:

Go back to the beginning of this story and try another path? **P1**

Or

Check out the list of choices? **P90**

You have decided to try to rescue the dog.

You squeeze under the lowest rail and wiggle as close as you can to the rope the dog is balancing on. Its body quivers in terror, and looks up at you with fearful brown eyes. You hook your leg around the rail and stretch to reach her… closer and closer, you are nearly there. As your fingers brush against her collar your leg slips and you and the dog are falling into the sea.

The water knocks your breath away and you are barely aware of the cold as you hit the sea and go under. For a moment you think you will keep sinking and never breathe air again, but then you kick towards the surface and start to rise. As you come back up, spitting salt water and gasping, you see the ferry moving away with a line of faces looking back at you. Trixie is swimming beside you, her head held high and small paws paddling.

On board a figure hurls something – a life preserver! The doughnut shape flies through the air and lands with a smack not far from you, and it bobs up and down in the water. With a few strokes you reach it and gratefully pull it over your body. Now you can float easily, and you turn around in the water to look for the dog. She is not far away, but the waves block her from view every few seconds. The little pendant at her throat seems to shine in the water.

You kick towards her and she scrabbles her front paws onto the red plastic ring. If you stay together you can both be rescued. You lean toward her and she licks your face, probably happy that she can rest. Your hand brushes the pendant on her collar as you get a comfortable grip on the dog, and you hear a strange ringing noise.

You spin around in the water, trying to figure out where the noise is coming from. Seconds ago you could see the big ferry, but now it seems to have disappeared – you can't see it anywhere!

You almost don't hear a shout above the slap and slosh of water.

"Ahoy!"

A small sailing boat appears with a boy in it. The boat comes quickly across the water and pulls up beside you. You pass the dog to the boy, and then he hands you a rope.

"Pull yourself aboard," the boy says with a smile.

It is time to make a decision. Do you:

Climb into the boat? **P79**

Or

Stay out of the boat? **P78**

You have decided not to get into the boat.

You shake your head. "No, I don't want to get into your boat."

The boy looks at you as if you are crazy and then shrugs. The breeze catches his sails and he moves on, leaving you to tread water looking vainly for the ferry or a better rescue vessel. Your legs are cold and starting to go numb, but you are sure you can feel something twining about them...

Suddenly, a long tentacle emerges from the water and slides up your arm. It is the extremely rare giant squid – and you are not feeling lucky about finding one.

The arms of the giant squid slither across your skin and tighten around you. You gasp for air as it squashes you, and you struggle to pull yourself free, but the squid is strong and it tugs you down into the water. You hold your breath, but how long will you last as you're pulled deeper and deeper and the water goes dark?

How did you end up like this? If only you'd made different choices! If only you could start again!

Wait! You can! It is time to make a decision. Do you.

Start this story from the beginning? **P1**

Or

Go to the List of Choices? **P90**

Or

Try those Math problems? **P72**

You have decided to get in the boat.

Grabbing the rope, you clamber aboard while the boy keeps the boat stable by leaning over on the other side. Soon you are safe in the bottom of the little boat, your sodden clothes dripping as Trixie licks your face.

The boy grins and hands you a blanket – it is dirty and smelly, but it is also thick and warm. You feel instantly better as you pull it around you.

"My name is Nick," the boy says, and you introduce yourself too.

"This is Trixie – it's thanks to her I was in the water."

Trixie huddles in between your legs and you warm each other. Looking around, you see you are in a small, old fashioned wooden sailboat.

Inside the boat are more blankets and a couple of sacks. The boat's captain is about your age. He is tanned a dark brown and wears a dirty shirt and torn trousers with a piece of rope holding them up. His legs and arms are covered with bruises.

He looks like he might be going to a pirate-themed fancy dress party. From the way he is looking at you, Nick seems to find *you* just as curious.

"Where did you come from?" he asks.

You try to explain about the ferry you fell from, but he looks confused and doesn't seem to understand. He examines the life preserver for a few seconds, and then shrugs and gets to work with the boat. He puts the sail up and it soon catches the breeze.

As you look at the hills on the nearby island you see that the farmland isn't there anymore – there are dense trees instead. Here and there are rough-looking houses with smoke rising from their chimneys.

Further down the channel you see some large masted sailboats. There is no sign of the ferry, and somehow the world seems quieter.

"Where do you want to go?" asks Nick.

"Nick, what year is it?

He laughs. "Are you mad? It's 1895, of course. Did you bump your head?"

So… you're in a little boat in a huge channel of water over a hundred years earlier than when you woke up this morning.

"I don't know where I need to go because I don't know anyone here, or at least, not in this time."

Nick laughs again, and shakes his head. "I don't have anywhere to go, either," he says. "I've run away from my uncle because he was always beating me."

Great, you think. *Both his parents are dead, and mine haven't been born yet.*

"So, *if* you went back in time, how do you think you did it?" Nick asks.

You explain about how you fell out of a large boat when you tried to rescue the dog. That you were thrown the life preserver and then… Then you touched the dog's collar.

You both stare at the dog at the bottom of the boat. Nick leans forward, one hand on your knee, and he pats Trixie's head.

"She seems a pretty ordinary dog. What about this?"

As he touches the strange pendant on her collar the sail boat lurches violently. When it steadies again you look about, there is still the sea and the boat but…

"Hey – Fowler's farm is gone!"

You don't know which farm that was, but it looks like some of the houses on the hill might have disappeared. One thing that's for sure is that the larger boats you saw before are gone. Now there is only one.

"Well I never," says Nick. "It's the *Endeavour* – one of the first ships from Europe to come to this land. Captain Cook sailed the *Endeavour* to New Zealand more than a hundred years ago. Cook wasn't the first European to see New Zealand, but he was the first to explore it, and he found this channel between the North and South Islands."

So… now you're in a little boat in a huge channel of water over *two hundred* years earlier than when you woke up this morning.

A longboat is lowered from the side of the *Endeavour.* Four sailors deftly climb ropes from the ship onto the longboat, and then row toward you. They look around as though they expect to see another boat or signs of life – but it is only you and Nick.

As they pull up beside you, one of the sailors pulls out a musket and trains it on you. You hold up your hands to show you aren't armed, and they look you over.

"Are you French?" one asks.

"No," says Nick, "we're lost. Can we come with you? I'm a good sailor."

You notice he isn't saying anything about time travel, and you decide you won't say anything either.

The sailors look inside your boat and seem surprised at the sight of Trixie. With help from a grappling hook and a rope they tow you back to the *Endeavour* where you climb aboard to meet the captain.

The captain's cabin has a low ceiling and it is full of plants, so it's like walking into an indoor forest or a greenhouse. You are led to a table, where Captain Cook has been writing. He wears a blue jacket and a white wig. He has a commanding presence and you hope he will treat you kindly. He looks you both up and down and you know he has taken a full measure of you both. This is an intelligent man. He speaks at last.

"My men tell me they have found you on the water alone – who are you, and what are you doing here?"

"We've been adrift for many days after we lost our ship in the islands," Nick says.

The captain looks at you for a long moment. "I do not know where you two came from, but from the look of you... " He turns to Nick and eyes his bruises "– it cannot have been a pleasant place. You are many, many days' sailing from civilization, and yet your dog seems well fed and neither of you are wasting from the scurvy. So let's put you to work."

"We can stay with you?" Nick seems incredibly happy as Captain Cook nods.

"You know these islands?" asks the Captain.

Nick chats away happily about the channel and the islands.

You have little to say – you have no knowledge of these waters and you are very aware of the differences between you and Nick.

He is happy to be here, to be useful and to have escaped his uncle, but you feel completely out of time and realize that while Nick will probably thrive you have few skills to help you get by.

As Nick talks, you rise and make your way to the captain's desk – there are charts neatly filed away and a large map is being drawn of the area. There are books about plants, and someone has been drawing the plants that fill the little cabin.

"Do you read?"

You realize this last question is being addressed to you.

"Of course!" you blurt out, before you remember that not everyone would have been able to read and write at this time in history.

"Can you reckon?"

Reckon? What's that? Ahhh, he means maths! You nod.

"Well, that explains your soft hands!" Captain Cook exclaims. "I will tell Banks that I have found him an assistant – and I have found myself an extra sailor."

Perhaps you won't be entirely useless in this place that you've wound up in. Joseph Banks is a botanist on the *Endeavour* and it was he who has filled it with plants. He is busy cataloguing all these new specimens.

A clanging noise announces that lunch is ready, and the captain sends you both to eat. On the way, you hurriedly discuss your situation with Nick. The dog keeps close to you both.

"If we touch that dog's collar again we could end up here a century before now," Nick says.

"Or maybe we'll go back to our own time!"

Nick shakes his head. "I don't want to go back!"

You think it through. When you first went back in time it was about a hundred years. The next time, Nick was touching both the medallion and you, and the boat and you and Nick all went back another hundred years. What would happen if somebody touched it again?

At that moment a sailor plucks up the little dog, and before you can do anything he touches the pendent. The ship lurches violently, creaks, and then steadies in the water. The sailors look around, trying to work out what has happened. They look overboard – perhaps they hit a rock or a whale. You and Nick look to the hills. At first everything seems the same, but then Nick gasps and points upwards.

Circling in the sky is the biggest bird you have ever seen.

"Haast's eagle!" says Nick. "They died out a long time ago. Oh no!"

"What is going on?" The captain comes up on deck and looks at everyone for an answer. Most of the crew are pointing to the giant eagle whose wings from tip to tip are wider than a man is tall.

The sailor is still holding Trixie, and to your horror his hand brushes the swinging medallion once more. Again the ship lurches, and the huge eagle disappears. The sailor drops the dog and she runs toward you. Trixie jumps into your arms and buries her nose in your shirt.

There is a bumping against the hull, and two of the sailors move to see what it is. You wonder if the next creature you will meet will be a giant shark. One of the sailors leans a little over the side and shakes his head.

"It was only the little sail boat," he says.

Wait! If the boat you and Nick arrived on is outside the ship, maybe that means you have gone FORWARD in time!

Once more you find yourself in the cabin of Captain Cook. He listens as you explain where you have come from, how you met Nick, and how the *Endeavour* has moved back and forward in time.

"The talisman is dangerous," Cook says, glaring at Trixie. "I don't want it on my ship. You must make a choice – you can throw it overboard now and stay with the *Endeavour*, or you can try to journey back to your own time in Nick's boat."

"I want to stay," Nick says.

It is time to make a decision. Do you:

Stay in this time? **P87**

Or

Try to return to your own time? **P88**

You've decided to stay in this time.

After thinking about it for a while, you decide that it's too risky to try to get back to your own time – who knows where (or when) you might end up.

You take Trixie's collar off and drop it into the deep waters of what will become known as the Cook Strait.

Later that day, you begin working with Joseph Banks. He is an enthusiastic and interesting man, and before long you discover that you too are passionate about botany. Together you travel the world, discovering new species of flora and fauna, and you make more of the world known to people. You live comfortably and Joseph treats you like one of his own children – he is a rich man, and he buys you a home and gives you all you need to be wealthy in your own right. You feel that the work you do leaves something for the future when people will appreciate the environment differently.

You live a long life, make many friends, and always have one of Trixie's descendants by your side.

Congratulations you've reached the end of this part of the story. But have you tried all the possible paths?

It is time to make one more decision. Do you:

Go to the list of choices? **P90**

Or

Go back to the beginning and try another path? **P1**

You have decided to try to return to your own time.

You farewell Nick and Captain Cook, and clamber down into the little boat. Nick carefully lowers Trixie down to you in a basket. You clumsily row a short distance from the *Endeavour* and then pick up Trixie.

If you have this wrong you could be about to go back one hundred years to a time when Maori is the only language spoken in this land, and giant birds ruled the skies…

You touch the pendant and the boat rocks, and you lose your grip on Trixie. You look up, scanning the sky for giant eagles, but seagulls are all you see. With relief you see sail boats in the distance – you went forward in time!

Now to try it again – well, the worst thing that can happen is you have to flag down the *Endeavour* again…

The boat tosses and…

Success! The ferry is instantly in sight, and within half an hour the ship has stopped and picked you up. You are congratulated by some passengers for rescuing the dog, but others are very grumpy that your falling overboard means that the ferry will arrive late.

"Thank you so much for rescuing my Trixie," her owner says. "But where has her collar gone?"

"I'm sorry – it must have been lost in the water," you say.

Trixie's owner seems upset, and you understand that she knew Trixie had been carrying a treasure.

Later, you tell Max and Stella about what happened, but

of course, they don't believe you. It doesn't matter, though, because in your back pocket you have something that would change their mind. Just for now you are keeping it for yourself – if you ever need to leap back in time, you'll be prepared.

Congratulations you have reached the end of this part of the story.

It is time to make another decision. Do you:

Go back to the beginning of this story and try another path? **P1**

Or

Go to the List of Choices? **P90**

List of Choices

(continued next page)

Answers

Question One:

A New Zealand giant squid can drag someone your weight and strength down to the bottom of a three mile trench in ten minutes. How many minutes would it take for two giant squid to drag you down to a watery grave?

Solutions: Adding more giant squid to the problem won't make them go any faster. If you assumed squid speed to be constant and guessed ten minutes you are a smart cookie. However, if two giant squid come across a tasty morsel like you they aren't going to share. While they fight over who gets to eat you, you should swim to safety or tie their tentacles into knots. A completely brilliant solution might be to point out that a creature that lives so far beneath the ocean wouldn't survive up on the surface and wouldn't be hunting there – but why ruin a good math problem.

Question Two:

You find a device which moves you backwards and forwards in time. You find out that you move back one hundred years every time you hit the back button and you move forward fifty years every time you hit the forward button. You travel back 300 years and find yourself being chased by a giant eagle. The Haast's eagle was the largest eagle ever known to have lived and has been extinct for two hundred years. How many times do you have to hit the forward button to avoid being a meal for a giant eagle?

Solutions: If the Haast eagle has been extinct for two hundred years and you have gone back in time three hundred years you only need to go forward 100 years to be safe from these giant predators. You move ahead fifty years each time you hit the forward button so you'll need to press it at least twice to be safe. If you want to get back to the present, you need to hit the button another four times.

Question Three:

While Lost in Lion Country you find yourself left alone with the safari picnic basket. There are 50 ham sandwiches inside the basket. One hyena will be satisfied after 10 ham sandwiches and will head off to sleep in the sun. How many hyena can you hold off until help arrives?

Solutions: Strictly speaking the answer is five but what if there are more hyena than that? We think a better solution is to empty out all but a few of the sandwiches into a pile for the pack to fight over. Take a couple yourself and a) if the picnic hamper is very sturdy consider getting inside until help arrives or b) climb up the nearest tree, have lunch, and wait for rescue.

Go to Arapawa Island **P2**
Or
Look at the List of Choices for stories you might have missed **P90**

More You Say Which Way Adventures.

Lost In Lion Country

Between the Stars

Danger on Dolphin Island

In the Magician's House

Secrets of Glass Mountain

Volcano of Fire

Once Upon an Island

The Sorcerer's Maze - Adventure Quiz

The Sorcerer's Maze - Jungle Trek

YouSayWhichWay.com

Special previews of more 'You Say Which Way' adventures

Preview: The Creepy House

Shhh! What's that noise?

Your family got a cheap deal on a bigger house, and the day you move in you find out why. Right next door is a creepy old place that looks like the set for a horror movie. Your family says it has character but you think it might have rats .... or worse.

Your cat is locked in the spare room while the movers are going in and out so she doesn't get lost. The cat was a bribe from your family to accept moving across town away from all your friends. She's small and gray and came from the animal shelter. You've thought of the perfect name for her: Ghost.

After the movers have gone and the doors are shut downstairs you let Ghost out to explore her new home. She comes into your room as you are putting away the last of your books and jumps on your bed.

"Hello Ghost. Do you like your new home?"

You settle down next to her with your book. It's called *Between the Stars* and it's about a weird space ship of sleeping travelers who wake up for adventures. It's really good but you are gradually distracted by a tapping at the window. That's odd, it's a second story window.

There's a tall tree just outside, it must be making the noise. You open the window and see that a branch is caught on some old wires. You untangle the wires just as you hear "Dinner's ready!" from downstairs. Your stomach growls, you don't need telling twice.

When you come back Ghost isn't on your bed anymore and you can feel a breeze from the open window. As you start to shut it you see your cat disappearing inside a window next door. She has climbed through the tree over to that spooky house.

"Ghost! Ghost! Puss, puss, puss!"

Through tattered drapes you can make out an old fashioned bed over there. A movement in the opposite room catches your eye and then you recognize yourself reflected in a long grimy mirror. You shiver a little. There's no sign of Ghost.

It is time to make your first decision. Do you:

Go over to the house and try to get your cat back?

Or

Leave the window open and wait for her to return?

Preview: The Sorcerer's Maze - Jungle Trek

One moment you were at home reading a book and now you are standing in the jungle, deep in the Amazon rainforest.

Beside you flows a slow-moving river, murky brown from all the silt it carries downstream. You hear monkeys screeching in the tall trees across the water. The air is hot and buzzing with insects. As you watch, the tiny flying creatures gather together in an unnatural cloud formation and then separate to form words:

WELCOME they spell in giant letters.

This is crazy you think.

NOPE, IT'S NOT CRAZY spell the insects. THIS IS THE START OF THE SORCERER'S MAZE.

Then the insect cloud bursts apart and the tiny creatures buzz off. What's next you wonder?

Twenty yards away two kids, about your age, stand beside a small boat with a little outboard motor attached to its stern. The boat has a blue roof to protect its occupants from the hot tropical sun.

They both smile and wave.

The girl walks towards you. "Do you want a ride up river?" she asks. "My brother and I know the Amazon well."

"Do you work for the sorcerer?" you ask. "He designed the maze, didn't he?"

The girl nods. "Yes. My brother and I are his apprentices.

The sorcerer wants you to have company while you're here."

The two of you walk back down to the river's edge.

"This is Rodrigo. I'm Maria."

You drop your daypack into the dugout and hold out your hand. "Hi Rodrigo, interesting looking boat."

Rodrigo shakes your hand. "It does the job. But before we can go upriver," he says, pulling a piece of paper out of his pocket. "The sorcerer wants me to ask you a question. If you get it right, we can leave."

"And if not?" you ask.

"I've got more questions," the boy says, patting his pocket. "I'm sure you'll get one right eventually." He unfolds the paper. "Okay, here's your first question. Which of the following statements is true?"

It is time to make a decision. Which do you choose?

The Amazon River has over 3000 known species of fish.

Or

The Amazon River has less that 1000 known species of fish.

Preview: In the Magician's House

You can't remember a time when you didn't live and work in the Magician's house. It is cloaked in mystery and you explore it every day.

There are many rooms, but you have to catch them while you can.

You find the kitchen easily most mornings. You just follow the lovely smells and don't think too hard about it. Perhaps your recent dreams help you get to breakfast without much trouble. More likely it's because the Magician wants his breakfast – why would he hide a place he wants you to go to?

You can find a lot of places in the house, especially the rooms you know about. You also have a knack for finding rooms you've never been to before and for this reason you're often asked to fetch things by the others who work in the house. They seem to get lost far more often than you do. You sometimes find other servants in the corners of rooms and give them a friendly pat to bring them out of a 'drawing room dream'. That is what the cook, Mrs Noogles, calls them. Dreams swirl around in the Magician's house just like dust does in the corners of other houses. Little stories get stuck in the crannies. Just for a moment, while you are sweeping a corner, you can find yourself running across a green field, speaking to a great crowd, steering an iron horse through twisty roads, or picking ripe strawberries in a bright warm field. Those are the dreams and they are quickly over, but other times you are transported to different places. So you watch where you step.

It is very early in the morning, and you wake up in your turret. It is your own tower above the house with a winding staircase that connects you to the house.

There is something cold against your cheek. You put your hand out and feel a smooth hard object. It's that frog again.

You open your eyes and see the red frog staring at you. You lift it from the pillow and place it next to a water filled glass bowl on a shelf. The rest of the shelf contains treasures and oddities that you've picked up, and some, like the frog, that seem to have followed you home. The frog sits perfectly still and turns to stone, but you know it is likely to change back and follow you like a naughty puppy. No matter – it's harmless and has never gotten you into trouble. You just hope you don't tread on it by accident one day when it isn't a stone.

The sky is dark purple, with one last star valiantly blinking as the rising sun starts to turn your corner of the world into day. You love looking out of your tower window and catching the day starting like this – in this moment the whole world is magic, not just the place you live.

Down the spiral staircase, on the next floor, you wash the sleep from your eyes and put on fresh clothes. A sound like a marble falling down the stairs becomes the sound of a rubber ball until the red frog appears with a final splat. He takes a quick dip in the big jug of water you keep for him there. When he jumps out he doesn't leave any wet marks on the flagstone floor. He seems to absorb moisture. The jug is now only half full and you top it up.

By the window, a row of ants are marching across the floor. The frog jumps over to the row of insects, and whips out his tongue to catch ant after ant until the column is gone. If only getting your breakfast was that easy.

From the window you can see the buildings of London- St Paul's cathedral is a beautiful dome by the river Thames. You see horses and carts making their deliveries down the twisty lanes. Much of London is still sleeping but servants are stirring to light the fires and make their master's breakfasts. You must tend to your master too.

As you move further down the turret you wonder which room it will join with today. Sometimes it will deliver you to a hallway which easily gets you to the servant's staircase and down to the kitchen but often there is another destination at the foot of the stairs. Things are seldom as they appear. You have learned to be cautious in case you step in a lily pond in the wide conservatory or walk into the shiny suit of armor which appears in different places each day.

The stairs wind down until you meet up with the rest of the house. Here is where you are usually faced with your first choice for the day. This morning a wide corridor stretches off to the left and right. The ceilings are high and arched. Embroidered tapestries hang along the oak paneled walls.

To your left, the corridor ends abruptly. A suit of armor stands at the dead end, its bright metallic form is leaning slightly forward, its gloved hand is holding up the edge of the last tapestry. Behind the tapestry, you can see the corner of what looks like a small door.

In the corridor to your right is an impassable hole in the floor with a ladder poking out. The carpet is ripped and torn around the hole as though a bomb has gone off in the night. That's weird, you think, you didn't hear an explosion.

You have never seen this hole or the secret door behind the tapestry before.

It's time to make your first decision for the day. Do you:

Go down the ladder into the hole?

Or

Take the secret door behind the suit of armor?

Preview: Secrets of Glass Mountain

With the screech of diamonds on smooth black rock, a troop of Highland Sliders comes skidding to a stop ten yards from you and your schoolmates.

"That's what I want to do when I leave school," says Dagma. "Being a Highland Slider looks like so much fun."

Another classmate shakes his head. "Yeah, but my cousin went mining and struck it rich on his first trip out. Now he owns two hydro farms and his family live in luxury."

You look around the small settlement where you grew up. It's a beautiful place, high on the Black Slopes of Petron. Far below, past the sharp ridges and towering pinnacles, the multicolored fields of the Lowlands stretch off into the distance. At the horizon, a pink moon sits above a shimmering turquoise sea.

But the beauty isn't enough to keep you here. You could never be a farmer or a merchant. You've always dreamed of travel and adventure.

Maybe mining is the right thing to do. You imagine heading off into the wild interior looking for diamonds and the many secrets these glass mountains contain. Imagine striking it rich!

Or do you become a slider like so many others from your family? What would happen to your home without the protection of the Highland Sliders? How would people move around the dangerous slopes from settlement to settlement without their expert guidance? And who would stop the Lowlanders from invading?

Your part in this story is about to begin. You will leave school at the end of the week and it's time for you to choose your future.

It is time to make your first decision. Do you:
Start cadet training to become a slider?
Or
Go to mining school so you can prospect for diamonds?

Preview: Pirate Island

Your family is on holiday at a lush tropical island resort in the Caribbean. But you're not in the mood to sit around the pool with the others, you want to go exploring. You have heard that pirate treasure has been found in these parts and you are keen to find some too. With a few supplies in your day pack, you fill your drinking bottle with water, grab your mask and snorkel, and head towards the beach.

You like swimming, but you've been planning this treasure hunt for months and now is as good a time as any to start. The beach outside the resort stretches off in both directions. To your right it runs past the local village, where children laugh as they splash and play in the water. Palm trees line the shore and brightly colored fishing boats rest on the sand above the high tide mark. Past the village, way off in the distance, is a lighthouse.

To your left, the sandy beach narrows quickly and soon becomes a series of rocky outcrops jutting into the sea. Steep cliffs rise up from the rocky shore to meet the stone walls of an old and crumbling fortress.

You have four hours before your family expect you back.

It is time to make your first decision. Do you:
Go right and head towards the lighthouse?
Or:
Go left and head towards the rocks and the old fortress?

Preview: Between the Stars.

You are in a sleep tank on the space ship *Victoria*. Your dreaming cap teaches you as you float.

You first put on a dreaming cap for the space sleep test. Although you thought it looked like you had an octopus on your head, you didn't joke about it. Nobody did. Everyone wanted to pass the test and go to the stars. Passing meant a chance to get out of overcrowded Londinium. If you didn't pass you'd likely be sent to a prison factory in Northern Europa. Nobody wanted to go there, even though Britannica hasn't been a good place lately, Europa was said to be worse.

When the judge sentenced you to transportation for stealing that food, you sighed inside with relief. You knew transportation was the chance of a better life on a faraway planet, but only if you passed the sleep test.

You lined up with other hopefuls and waded into a pool of warm sleep jelly. They were all young like you and they all looked determined.

"Stay calm," the robot instructed. "Breathe in slowly through your mouthpiece and relax."

Nearby, a young woman struggled from the pool. She pulled out her breathing plug and gasped for breath.

"Take her back," said a guard. You knew what that meant – back to prison and then the factories. A convict sneered at the poor girl, the cruel look on his face magnified by a scar running down one cheek.

In your short time in prison, you had learned there were people who would have been criminals no matter what life they'd been born to. Something told you that he was one of them.

You put him out of your mind and concentrated on doing what the robot said. You thought of the warm porridge you'd had every morning in the orphanage growing up. The sleeping jelly didn't seem so strange then. When your head was submerged you breathed in slowly.

As the jelly filled your lungs you fought against thoughts of drowning. You'd listened at the demonstration and knew it was oxygenated. *This must be what it's like to be a fish*, you'd thought as you moved forward through the thick fluid, *I only have to walk through to the other side.*

Closing your eyes, you moved forward through the thick warm jelly. "Relax," you told yourself. "You can do this."

You opened your eyes just in time to see the scar-faced youth about to knock your breather off. Thankfully the jelly slowed his punch and you ducked out of the way just in time. Then a moment later, you were on the other side being handed a towel.

"This one's a yes," intoned a man in a white coat. He slapped a bracelet on your wrist and sent you down a corridor away from your old life. As you exited, you just had time to hear the fate of the scar-faced youth. "He'll do. Take him to the special room."

Days of training followed. You often joined other groups of third class passengers but you didn't see Scar-Face among them. You passed all the tests and then one day, you got into a sleep tank beside hundreds of others. Your dreaming cap would teach you everything you'd need to know in your new life.

You were asleep when the *Victoria* was launched into space. You slept as the *Victoria* lost sight of the Earth and then its star, the sun.

And here you are, years later, floating in sleep fluid and learning with your dreaming cap. Or you were. Because now you hear music. Oxygen hisses into your sleeping chamber and the fluid you have been immersed in starts to drain away. Next time you surface, you'll breathe real air, something that your lungs haven't done in a long time.

"Sleeper one two seven six do you accept this mission? Sleeper, please engage if you wish to awaken for this mission. Sleeper, there are other suitable travelers for this mission. Do you choose to wake?"

Passengers can sleep the entire journey if they want. They can arrive at the new planet without getting any older. First class passengers will own land and riches when they arrive but you are third class, you have nothing. Groggily, you listen to the voice. If you choose to take on a mission you can earn credit for the new planet – even freedom – but you could also arrive on the new planet too old to ever use your freedom.

"Sleeper, do you accept the mission?"

It is time to make your first decision.
Do you want to wake up and undertake this mission?
Or
Do you wait for a different mission or wait to land on the new planet?

Preview: Lost in Lion Country

You only jumped out of the Land Rover for a second to take a photo. How did the rest of your tour group not notice? You were standing right beside the vehicle taking photos of a giraffe. It's not like you walked off somewhere.

The next thing you know, dust is flying and you are breathing exhaust fumes as the Land Rover races off after the pride of lions your group has been following all morning.

'Wait for me!' you scream as loud as you can. 'Wait for me!'

Unfortunately, the sound of the revving diesel engine drowns out your cries. Surely one of your family members on the safari will notice you are missing. Maybe that nice teacher lady from Chicago you were chatting to earlier will wonder where you are. Won't the driver realize he's one person short?

You smack yourself on the forehead. This will teach you for sitting alone in the back row while the others on the safari sat up front to hear the driver's commentary.

'This is not good,' you say to yourself.

What are you going to do now? It's just as well you packed a few emergency supplies in your daypack before you boarded the tour. You have bottled water, a couple of sandwiches, a chocolate bar, your pocket knife and your trusty camera. But these things won't help you if you are seen by hungry lions, leopards, cheetah or one of the other predators that stalk the savannah.

With the vehicle now only a puff of dust in the distance, you notice something else much closer, a pack of hyenas. These scavengers weren't a problem when you were in the vehicle, but now you are on foot and the hyenas are heading your way!

You know from all the books on African wildlife you've read, these dog-like animals can be vicious and have been known to work as a team to bring down much larger animals. They would have no problem making short work of you if they wanted to.

If they find you out here all alone in the Serengeti National Park, you will be in big trouble.

You look around. What should you do? You know that normally the thing to do when you get lost is to stay put so others can find you when they come looking, but the hyenas make that impossible.

Off to your right is a large acacia tree that you might be able to climb, while on your left is a dried up creek bed.

With the hyenas getting closer you have to move.

You decide to run over and climb up the large acacia tree

The giraffe has moved off to look for more tasty leaves. As you head towards the acacia tree, you keep looking over your shoulder at the pack of hyenas to see if they have spotted you. Luckily, the pack is upwind so their keen noses may have not picked up your scent yet, especially with all the wildebeest and zebra in the area. Still, they are covering the ground faster than you are.

The hyenas are funny looking animals. Unlike dogs, their front legs are slightly longer than their back legs, causing them to slope up towards their head. The members of this pack have light brown bodies with black spots, black faces, and funny rounded ears. If you weren't so afraid of getting eaten by them, you'd stop and take photos.

You are nearly at the tree when one of the hyenas perks up its ears and yips to the others. Suddenly the whole pack is running as fast as they can right at you!

There is no time to waste. You run as fast as you can towards the tree and start looking for a way up. Luckily you can just reach one of the lower branches. You pull yourself up by clamping your legs around the trunk and grabbing every hand hold the tree offers. Once you are up on the first limb, the climbing gets easier.

The hyenas are under the tree now, eagerly yipping to each other. A couple of scrawny looking ones take a run at the tree and jump, snapping at your legs. You pull your legs up, and climb a little higher. They circle the tree and stare up at you with their black beady eyes. You are trapped.

You take off your daypack and slip out your camera. No point in missing a great photo opportunity just because you're in a spot of danger. After taking a couple shots you pull out your water bottle and have a little sip. You don't want to drink too much because you are not sure when you'll find more. The grasses on the savannah are turning brown, so you doubt there has been much rain recently. You can see down into the creek from here and it looks bone dry.

Some of the hyenas lay down in the shade of the tree. Their tongues hang out of their mouths. Are they going to wait you out? Do they think you will fall?

You remember reading that hyenas hunt mainly at night. Are they going to hang around in the shade until sundown? How will your family find you if you have to stay up here?

You could be in for a long wait and try to make yourself comfortable. After wedging your backside in between two branches and hooking your elbow around another, you start to think about what to do to get out of this situation.

It is pretty obvious that climbing down and running for it would be a really bad idea. The pack of hyena would have you for lunch before you could get five steps. Maybe when they realize they can't get to you, the pack will move on. Or maybe they will see something that is more likely to provide them with an easy meal.

Just as you are about to lose hope, you see a dust cloud in the distance. It is getting bigger. Is the dust cloud being caused by animals or is it the Land Rover coming back for you?

You stand up and look through the leaves and shimmering haze rising from the grassy plain. Further out on the savannah thousands of wildebeest are on the move.

Surely the cloud is moving too fast to be animals. Then you see the black and white Land Rover owned by the safari tour company. But will they see you? The track is quite some distance away from the tree you are in. You didn't realize you'd come so far.

You scold yourself for not leaving something in the road to mark your position. You yell and wave and wish you'd worn bright clothing so the others could see you through the spindly leaves, but the Land Rover isn't stopping. It drives right past your position and races off in the other direction.

'Come back!' you yell.

You sit down again and think. What can you do? It looks like you are on your own, for now at least.

Then you remember the sandwiches in your daypack. Maybe the hyenas would leave you alone if you gave them some food? But then what happens if they don't leave and you're stuck up the tree for a long time and get hungry?

A pair of vultures land in the bleached branches of a dead tree not far away. Do they know something you don't?

It is time to make a decision. Do you:

Throw the hyenas your sandwiches and hope they will eat them and leave?

Or

Keep your food for later and prepare for a long wait?

Preview: Volcano of Fire

You sit at a long table in the command pod atop one of the twin Pillars of Haramon. The room is filled with the hum of voices. A small robotic bird, unseen by those in the room, hovers in one corner.

The man at the head of the table has three blue-diamond stars pinned to his chest, indicating his rank as chief of the council. Next to him sits a visiting Lowland general, his face as hard as the rock walls of the command pod. Around the table, other important figures from both the Highlands and the Lowlands sit nervously.

Being the newest member of the Highland Council, you have yet to earn your first star, but you have big plans to make your mark.

"Quiet please," the chief says. "We've got important matters to discuss."

The chief's scars are visible, even from your seat at the opposite end of the table. These scars are proof of the many battles and expeditions he has taken part in over his long career and are proof of the dangers of living in the Highlands where the rock under your feet is the slipperiest material imaginable. Black glass.

"Supplies of tyranium crystals have run desperately low," the chief says. "Without tyranium, workers can't move safely around the slopes and that means no progress on the trade routes being built between the Lowlands and the Highlands.

If our truce is to last, trade is critical."

As you listen to the chief talk, you stare out of the large windows that overlook the slopes below. Further down Long Gully, the second pillar rises from the smooth black slope. A colony of red-beaked pangos squabble with each other for nesting spaces in the cracks near its summit.

To the south are the patchwork fields of the Lowlands, the blue ribbons of the river delta and the turquoise sea. Petron's smallest moon has just risen, pale pink in the morning light, just above the horizon.

"We need to mount an expedition to locate a new source of crystals, and soon," the chief says. "Led by someone we trust."

He turns and looks in your direction. "Someone who knows how to slide on black glass and has the ability to lead a team. Someone with a knowledge of mining and brave enough to take chances when necessary. Are you up for it?" the chief asks, catching you off guard.

"Me?" Sure you've been a troop leader in the Slider Corps and spent a little time in mining school, but leading an expedition into new territory? That's quite a responsibility.

The Lowland general stands, rests his hairy knuckles on the table before him, and leans towards your end of the table. "We need someone who is respected by both the Lowlanders and the Highlanders. Someone both sides trust to ensure an equal share of any discoveries."

"That's right," the chief says. "It was you who helped

start the peace process. You are the logical choice."

Your part in this story is about to begin. You are being asked to undertake a dangerous mission, one that is important to your community. But are you really qualified? You are young. Surely others would be more suitable. Maybe you should suggest someone more experienced lead the expedition, then you could go back home and live a safe life growing hydro or hunting pangos.

It is time to make your first decision. Do you:

Agree to lead the mission?

Or

Suggest someone else lead the mission?

Preview: Dangers of Dolphin Island

From the float plane's window, you can see how Dolphin Island got its name.

The Island looks like a dolphin leaping out of the water. A sparkling lagoon forms the curve of the dolphin's belly, two headlands to the east form its tail and to the west another forms the dolphin's nose. As the plane banks around, losing altitude in preparation for its lagoon landing, the island's volcanic cone resembles a dorsal fin on the dolphins back.

Soon every camera and cell phone is trained on the fiery mountain.

"Wow look at that volcano," shouts a kid in the seat in front of you. "There's steam coming from the crater."

The plane's pontoons kick up a rooster-tail of spray as they touch down on the lagoon's clear water. As the plane slows, the pilot revs the engine and motors towards a wooden wharf where a group of smiling locals await your arrival.

"Welcome to Dolphin Island," the resort staff say as they secure the plane, unload your bags, and assist you across the narrow gap to the safety of a small timber wharf.

Coconut palms fringe the lagoon's white-sand beach. Palm-thatched huts poke out of the surrounding jungle. The resort's main building is just beyond the beach opposite the wharf.

Between the wharf's rustic planks you can see brightly colored fish dart back and forth amongst the coral. You stop and gaze down at the world beneath your feet.

You hear a soft squeak behind you and step aside as a young man in cut-off shorts trundles past pushing a trolley with luggage on it. He whistles a song as he passes, heading towards the main resort building. You and your family follow.

"Welcome to Dolphin Island Resort," a young woman with a bright smile and a pink flower tucked behind her ear says from behind the counter as you enter the lobby. "Here is the key to your quarters. Enjoy your stay."

Once your family is settled into their beachfront bungalow, you're eager to explore the island. You pack a flashlight, compass, water bottle, pocket knife, matches, mask, snorkel and flippers as well as energy bars and binoculars in your daypack and head out the door.

Once you hit the sand, you sit down and open the guidebook you bought before coming on vacation. Which way should you go first? You're still a little tired from the early morning flight, but you're also keen to get exploring.

As you study the map, you hear a couple of kids coming towards you down the beach.

"Hi, I'm Adam," a blond haired boy says as he draws near.

"And I'm Jane."

The boy and girl are about your age and dressed in

swimming shorts and brightly colored t-shirts, red for him and yellow for her. They look like twins. The only difference is that the girl's hair is tied in a long ponytail while the boy's hair is cropped short. Both are brown and have peeling noses. By their suntans you suspect they've been at the resort a few days already.

"What are you reading?" Adam asks.

"It's a guide book. It tells all about the wildlife and the volcano. It also says there might be pirate treasure hidden here somewhere. I'm just trying to figure out where to look first."

Jane clasps her hands in front of her chest and does a little hop. "Pirate treasure, really?"

Adam looks a little more skeptical, his brow creases as he squints down at you. "You sure they just don't say that to get the tourists to come here?"

"No, I've read up on it. They reckon a pirate ship named the *Port-au-Prince* went down around here in the early 1800s. I thought I might go exploring and see what I can find."

"Oh can we help?" Jane says. "There aren't many kids our age staying at the moment and lying by the pool all day gets a bit boring."

"Yeah," Adam agrees. "I'm sure we could be of some help if you tell us what to do. I've got a video camera on my new phone. I could do some filming."

There is safety in numbers when exploring, and three sets of eyes are better than one. But if you do find treasure, do

you want to share it with two other people?
It is time to make your first decision. Do you:
Agree to take Adam and Jane along?
Or
Say no and go hunting for treasure on your own?

Preview: The Sorcerer's Maze

Your feet are sinking into a marshmallow floor. You take a few quick steps and find you can stay on top if you keep moving. How did you get here? One moment you were reading and now you are in a long hallway. The place smells of candy and the pink walls are soft when you poke them.

There is a sign hanging from the ceiling that says: YOU ARE AT THE BEGINNING OF THE SORCERER'S MAZE. But how do you get through to the end of the maze? That is the big question.

Down at the end of the hallway is an old red door. Maybe you should start there?

You take a few bouncy steps, your arms held out to help keep your balance. Getting up would be hard. You don't want to fall.

At last you make it to the red door and try the doorknob. It's locked. You pace in a circle to stop from sinking. When you turn back to the door you find another sign. On this sign is a question. Below the question are two possible answers. Maybe answering the question correctly will let you open the door.

The questions reads: What is the largest planet in our solar system?

It's time to make your first decision. You may pick right, you may pick wrong, but still the story will go on. What shall it be?

Jupiter? Or Saturn?

Preview: Dragons Realm

"Hey, Fart-face!"

Uh oh. The Thompson twins are lounging against a fence as you leave the corner store – Bart, Becks, and Bax. They're actually the Thomson triplets, but they're not so good at counting, so they call themselves twins. Nobody has dared tell them different.

They stare at you. Bart, big as an ox. Becks, smaller but meaner. And Bax, the muscle. As if they need it.

Bart grins like an actor in a toothpaste commercial. "What have you got?" He swaggers towards you.

Becks sneers, stepping out with Bax they close behind. "Come on, squirt, hand it over," she calls, her meaty hands bunching into fists.

Your backpack is heavy with goodies. Ten chocolate bars and two cans of tuna fish for five bucks – how could you resist? And now you could lose it all.

The twins form a human wall, blocking the sidewalk. There's no way around them.

Seriously? All this fuss over chocolate? Not again! They've been bullying you and your friends for way too long. There's still time to outsmart them before the bus leaves for the school picnic.

A girl walks between you and the twins. You make your move, sprinting off towards the park next to school. Your backpack is heavy, but you've gained a head start on those numb skulls.

Becks roars.

"Charge," yells Bax,

"Get the snot-head," Bart bellows. Their feet pound behind you as you make it around the corner through the park gate. Now to find a hiding place.

On your right is a thick grove of trees. They'll never find you in there, not without missing the bus to the picnic.

To your left, is a sports field. Behind the bleachers, there's a hole in the fence. If you can make it through that hole, you're safe. They're much too big to follow.

Their pounding footsteps are getting closer. They'll be around the corner soon.

It is time to make a decision. Do you:

Race across the park to the hole in the fence?

Or

Hide from the Thompson twins in the trees?

(end of previews)

For more of each story go to:
Amazon.com and search for 'you say which way'.

You Say Which Way
Brought to you by:
The Fairytale Factory

Made in the USA
Middletown, DE
30 November 2015